"THE USUAL, AND TREASURED, NOLAN TRADEMARKS ARE HERE: characters defined through their actions; storylines that unfurl with alacrity and grace; expository description as concise as it is complete. Yet *Ships in the Night* is a Nolan book like no other, for its ten stories cover all the bases, encompassing several genres (Western, detective, sports, sci-fi) as well as that murkier area known as the human condition. The author's career thus is encapsulated in a single volume, for as Christopher Conlon observes in his Nolan Introduction (to *Dark Universe*, Stealth Press, 2001), Bill is 'one of our great literary ventriloquists…[his] style adjusts itself to each new plot and set of characters.'"

—PAUL McCOMAS

SHIPS
IN THE
NIGHT

Max Brand: Western Giant (anthology/bibliography, 1986)
Max Brand's Best Western Stories III (Brand collection, 1987)
Tales of the Wild West (Brand collection, 1997)
More Tales of the Wild West (Brand collection, 1999)
Masquerade (Brand collection, 2005)
King of the Pulps (biography, in progress)

On Dashiell Hammett
Dashiell Hammett: A Casebook (critical study, 1969)
Hammett: A Life at the Edge (biography, 1983)
A Life Beyond Thursday (biography, 2004)
Dash (stage play, 2004)

On Ray Bradbury
Ray Bradbury Review (anthology, 1952)
The Ray Bradbury Index (pamphlet, 1953)
The Ray Bradbury Companion (bio/bibliography, 1975)
The Dandelion Chronicles (pamphlet, 1984)
The Bradbury Chronicles (anthology, 1991)

Science Fiction Anthologies
The Pseudo-People (1965)
Man Against Tomorrow (1965)
Il Meglio Della Fantascienza (1967)
3 to the Highest Power (1968)
A Wilderness of Stars (1969)
A Sea of Space (1970)
The Future is Now (1970)
The Human Equation (1971)
Science Fiction Origins (1980)

Science Fiction Collections
Alien Horizons (1974)
Wonderworlds (1977)
Wild Galaxy (2005)

Bibliographies
The Work of Charles Beaumont (1986)
The Work of William F. Nolan (1988)
Have You Seen the Wind? (collection, with prose, 2003)
Ill Met by Moonlight (collection, with prose and artwork, 2004)

Verse
The Mounties (broadside, 1979)
Dark Encounters (collection, 1986)

Auto Racing Works
Omnibus of Speed (anthology, 1958)
Adventure on Wheels (John Fitch autobiography, 1959)
Barney Oldfield (biography, 1961)
Phil Hill: Yankee Champion (biography, 1962)
Men of Thunder (collection, 1964)
When Engines Roar (anthology, 1964)
Steve McQueen: Star on Wheels (biography, 1972)
Carnival of Speed (collection, 1973)

Horror Works
The Fiend in You (anthology, 1962)
Things Beyond Midnight (collection, 1984)
Urban Horrors (anthology, 1990)
How to Write Horror Fiction (reference, 1990)
Blood Sky (chapbook, 1991)
Helltracks (novel, 1991)
Night Shapes (collection, 1995)
William F. Nolan's Dark Universe (career collection, 2001)
Nightworlds (collection, 2004)

Miscellaneous Works
A Cross Section of Art in Science-Fantasy (chapbook, 1952)
Image Power (pamphlet, 1988)
Rio Renegades (Western novel, 1989)
California Sorcery (mixed anthology, 1999)
Simply An Ending (pamphlet, 2002)

With Marlowe in L.A. (pamphlet, 2003)

Other Collections
Impact 20 (mixed short stories, 1963)
The Edge of Forever (collection of Chad Oliver stories, 1971)
Down the Long Night (crime collection, 2000)
Offbeat (collection of Richard Matheson stories, 2002)

Other Biographies
John Huston: King Rebel (1965)
Sinners and Supermen (collection, 1965)
Hemingway: Last Days of the Lion (chapbook, 1974)
McQueen (1984)
The Black Mask Boys (collection/anthology, 1985)

Motion Pictures
The Legend of Machine-Gun Kelly (1975)
Logan's Run (1976)
Burnt Offerings (1976)

Television Works
Brain Wave (*One Step Beyond*, 1959)
Vanishing Act (*Wanted: Dead or Alive*, 1959)
Black Belt (*Wanted: Dead or Alive*, 1960)
The Joy of Living (*Norman Corwin Presents*, 1971)
The Norliss Tapes (NBC Movie of the Week, 1973)
The Turn of the Screw (ABC miniseries, 1974)
Trilogy of Terror (*Millicent and Therese; Julie*) (ABC Movie of the Week, 1975)
Sky Heist (NBC Movie of the Week, 1975)
The Kansas City Massacre (ABC Movie of the Week, 1975)
Logan's Run (pilot for CBS series, 1977)
First Loss (*240-Robert*, 1981)
The Partnership (*Darkroom*, 1981)
Terror at London Bridge (NBC Movie of the Week, 1985)
Trilogy of Terror II (*The Graveyard Rats; He Who Kills*) (USA Movie of the Week, 1996)

SHIPS
IN THE
NIGHT

AND OTHER STORIES

William F. Nolan

FOREWORD BY PAUL McCOMAS

CAPRA PRESS
MEMORABLE BOOKS SINCE 1969
SANTA BARBARA

Ships in the Night is a work of fiction. Names, places, characters, and incidents are either products of the author's imagination or used to further same. Any resemblance to actual events or to persons alive or dead is coincidental.

A Robert Bason Book
Published by Capra Press
155 Canon View Road
Santa Barbara, CA 93108
www.caprapress.com

Cover and book design by Frank Goad, Santa Barbara

Library of Congress Cataloging-in-Publication Data

Nolan, William F., 1928-
Ships in the night, and other Stories / by William F. Nolan ;
Foreword by Paul McComas.
p. cm.
"A Robert Bason Book."
ISBN 1-59266-049-5 (trade)
I. Title.
PS3564.O39S54 2003
813'.54—dc21
2003002389

Edition: 10 9 8 7 6 5 4 3 2 1

First Edition

This collection is dedicated to Robert Bason
for taking a chance.

"In a novel or play you must be a whole man. In a collection of stories you can be all the men or fragments of men, worthy and unworthy, who in different seasons abound within you. It is a luxury not to be scorned."

—IRWIN SHAW

CONTENTS

MAN OF MANY WORLDS
Foreword by Paul McComas

WHAT A PRIVILEGE IT IS to introduce William F. Nolan's remarkable new collection – and what an odd path it is that's led me here! In a way, I owe it all to a broken leg. Allow me to explain.

Like many "tweeners" (born in the early '60s, between the Baby Boom and Generation X), I first encountered Bill's work indirectly, through the 1976 film adaptation of his novel, *Logan's Run*. At fourteen, I was entranced by the movie's depiction of a flashy, flesh-laden future society; I remember musing that if I could spend my life hanging out in a space-age shopping center, zipping about in mazecars and casually bedding eager young lovelies, I wouldn't *mind* dying at thirty.*

---

* In Bill's novel the compulsory death age is twenty-one. In the new Warner Bros. remake (set for release in 2006), the novel's death age has been restored to twenty-one.

How devoted a Loganite was I? I saw the film six times the summer it was released and, later, watched and audio-taped each episode of the short-lived TV series (this was pre-VCR). For my fifteenth birthday, I took three friends to Milwaukee's Northridge Court where, toy flameguns in hand, we tracked and chased each other up and down the escalators and all across the mall (I "terminated" two Runners with a single blast outside Spencer Gifts). And when MGM failed to announce a follow-up film, I grabbed my trusty Minolta regular-8 and shot a sequel and two prequels of my own.

My interest in the film *Logan's Run* (which Bill has aptly described as "a good popcorn movie") inevitably led me to the 1967 source novel by Bill and coauthor George Clayton Johnson, and it was there – and in the Nolan-penned sequels – that I found the real deal. For this was narrative written to read at breakneck speed, propulsive, kinetic and lean…with rich and compelling themes. Indeed, Nolan's Logan cycle was and remains not only wildly imaginative, but also quite astute in its cautionary critique of recent societal trends and what they suggest about the shape of things to come.

But back to our story. In May 1977, a double spiral fracture I sustained while skateboarding deep-sixed my summer plans to earn a green belt in karate. So instead, while my cast-entombed tibia and fibula healed, I wrote and illustrated *The* Logan's Run *Referance* [sic] *Book*. Featuring "195 terms and 26 drawings in 23 big pages," my compendium of All Things Logan was "published" via the Xerox machine in my Dad's office; I then advertised it in Vol. II, No. 2 of *The Circuit*, official 'zine of the *Logan's Run* Organization of Fans. Lo and behold, among the thirty-odd people across the U.S. to dutifully mail me a $2 check was none other than William F. Nolan.

It was with jittery fingers that I packed up a copy of my concordance and sent it winging westward – and with equally jittery fingers that, a few weeks later, I opened and read Bill's handwritten reply. To my great relief, he'd found my booklet to be "a delight, lots of fun to read," and added, "For your age, I think you've done a wonderful job.... I, too, was writing in my teens (wrote my first short stories at 10 and my first novel at 15!). I think you show a lot of talent. Good luck...you have the Logan spirit!"

It meant the world to me that an accomplished professional author like William F. Nolan saw promise in my work – and that he would take the time to pick up his pen and tell me so. In a very real sense, it was at that moment that my literary career began. For in the days that followed, I stopped writing about Bill's narrative, *Logan's Run*, and began creating narratives of my own.

As I've been doing ever since.

Fast-forward to April 2002. I'm invited to perform some of my work at the World Horror Con in Chicago, and though I'm not really a horror writer, I accept. Thank God I do, for who should be slated to receive the International Horror Guild's Living Legend Award but William F. Nolan! I write to him in advance of the event, reminding him of our (much) earlier contact and thanking him for the encouragement, and

I enclose a copy of my published (*not* Xeroxed this time) short-story book, *Twenty Questions* (Daniel & Daniel, 1998). Bill writes right back: "Great hearing from you! Wow! 25 years! Delighted to see that your own writing career is well under way. If I was of help in 'kickstarting' it, then that's wonderful to know."

At the Horror Con, Bill accepts his award to a standing ovation, then greets me as he would a long-lost son, offering a pair of autographed books he has brought me from home and taking me out to dinner. He's in the front row the next morning when artist Chris Kozlowski and dancer Jamie Horban assist me in presenting two of my darker works onstage. I dedicate the pieces to Bill, and the gesture clearly touches him. That evening, I get to introduce Bill at his reading/discussion event at a local library. Afterward Chris and I take *him* out to dinner, during which he praises our performance and regales us with many a tale we'll not soon forget! (If ever you're fortunate enough to meet Bill, ask him to tell you "the mummy story.")

The next morning, while driving Bill to O'Hare Airport for his flight home, I ask whether he'd be willing to read my about-to-be-published novel, *Unplugged* (John Daniel & Co., 2002); he immediately assents, and three weeks later I hold in my hand the most eloquent and enthusiastic back-cover blurb a first-time novelist could ever hope to receive.

But it doesn't end there. One month later, I receive yet *another* piece of correspondence in that now-familiar script, namely a letter that begins, "Paul, ol' Scout! How'd you like to write the Intro to my next book of stories?"

Very much…thank you!

Which brings us – finally! – to the collection before you. Having just read it, I've much to report – all good. The usual, and treasured, Nolan trademarks are here: characters defined through their actions; storylines that unfurl with alacrity and grace; expository description as concise as it is complete. Yet *Ships in the Night* is a Nolan book like no other, for its ten stories cover all the bases, encompassing several genres (Western, detective, sports, sci-fi) as well as that murkier area known as the human condition. The author's career thus is encapsulated in a single volume, for as Christopher Conlon observes in *his* Nolan Introduction (to *Dark Universe,* Stealth Press, 2001), Bill is "one of our great literary ventriloquists…[his] style adjusts itself to each new plot and set of characters."

In this, Bill and I are kindred spirits, for I too have been credited with (and accused of) a kind of freewheeling, style-defying eclecticism. Thus, a question once flung at me by a puzzled publisher could be reframed for Bill: "Will the real William F. Nolan please stand up?"

In *Ships in the Night*, the answer rings out loud and clear: "They have!"

"Encounter with A King" uses the brutal drama of a boxing match to ask pointed questions about strength, character, and strength *of* character – ideals whose definitions prove fluid, elusive, even contradictory. In an ambiguous world, Nolan suggests, it may be possible to both find and forfeit oneself in, literally, a single blow.

The cinematic barnstorming tale "The Sky Gypsy" is,

first and foremost, a gripping adventure yarn, told with prose that swoops and soars like a Hisso Standard. But this is also a story about growing up, about learning to value what really matters in life, and about how wisdom is gained through experience – often at great cost to oneself or others.

"Of Time and Kathy Benedict" is the sole story told from a female point of view – quite plausibly, at that. Indeed, Nolan has crafted in Kathy a delightful heroine: a free spirit in search of a soulmate, open to adventure, savoring each twist and turn along the way. By dramatizing a near-death experience that paves the way for growth and love – the premise, coincidentally, of my novel *Unplugged*, about a woman not unlike Kathy – the story seems to say that we sometimes must let the old parts of ourselves perish to gain a new lease on life.

Nolan's ear for dialogue moves front and center in "Two Coffees," a pithy vignette about a salesman trying to sell salesmanship itself – but to someone who ain't buying. The rat-a-tat spiel of Sidney Lanham will be familiar to anyone who has "done time" (i.e., worked against their will) in marketing, advertising, retail or p.r. Life is full of sobering occasions when success and dignity turn out to be mutually exclusive, and "Two Coffees" sharply documents one such instance.

"Helle on Wheels" is a colorful cat-and-mouse detective story, as humorous as it is suspenseful, that encompasses everything from Civil War history to stunt driving, boxers-for-hire to buried treasure. Here, Nolan pulls out all the stops strictly, I believe, to entertain – and he fully succeeds, aided by a cast of characters so deftly drawn, they positively double-flip off the page.

I have a built-in affinity for the Western setting, and "Shadow Quest" certainly does that setting justice. The reader is transported: hear the wind whipping through the grassy terrain of the Sierra Madres; feel the fallen fir needles poking up from the forest floor; glimpse, by night, the "mass of tall pines that crowded the stars." On the surface, the story is about a wild man's pursuit of an even wilder horse; on a deeper level, it's about freedom. And if, at story's end, the protagonist does not acquit himself as I had hoped he would, it's simply because, between the author's vision and this reader's, Nolan's is the more realistic.

The auto racing tale "The Ragged Edge" is about fear: of failure, yes – but also of success. The consequences of winning, Nolan notes, can make for a heavy load, equal parts boon and burden. This story seems a companion piece to "Encounter with A King," for again, slippery questions about character pop up in the midst of a highly charged, highly public contest – one that is, in each case, exceedingly well-rendered. "The Ragged Edge" also calls to mind "Of Time and Kathy Benedict" in that both pieces have something to say about courage, love, and how each can bolster the other.

The father-and-son sketch "Just Like Wild Bob" depicts what's popularly known as a dysfunctional relationship, though Nolan uses far more artful words than those to bring parent and adult child to life and their uneasy bond to light. Is this a story about reconciliation – about paternal pride toppling a bulwark of bitterness? Before you decide, note that the line of dialogue from which the title is derived suggests a second interpretation, given what we've learned about Wild Bob at Elm Ridge – and that's the genius of this story. For this isn't necessarily a case of either/or: the father's statement just might carry with it both meanings at once.

Lyrical, poetic and somewhat enigmatic, "Ships in the Night" invokes the recollected moments of wallowing and wonder, of rapture and regret, of tragedy and transcendence that, braided together, comprise one man's life. The brush with death that sets the story into motion is appropriate, for old Harvey's subsequent list-making has to it elements not only of elegy but of eulogy. Haunted by his past, Harvey has, in a sense, stopped living; no longer *of* this world, he seems resigned simply to observe it, ghost-like, from the shadows.

And then there's "The Grackel Question," a wry and sly slice of sci-fi, recounted in the slang of its time (2179). After all these years, Nolan is clearly at home in this genre, tossing generous doses of humor and irony into the mix to goose the formula – and to keep the reader guessing. This futurefable ponders questions of mortality (curse or blessing?), morality (fixed or relative?) and, above all, identity – the drive to maintain one's self in an increasingly self-denying world. As usual, no matter how exotic the setting, how far-flung the year or how fanciful the window dressing (hitchies and Grackels and 'bugs, oh my!), Nolan's concerns ring true to our world, our culture, our times.

Varied though these ten tales be, when one considers

them together, common themes do emerge. For in reflecting on this collection, what words have I used? Character. Strength. Courage. Fear. Wisdom. Dignity. Freedom. Identity. This is an ambitious book, for in *Ships in the Night*, Nolan tackles no less a topic than humanity itself: our feats and our foibles, our hopes and our hardships, how we rise to – or shrink from – the myriad challenges life throws our way.

Twenty-seven years ago, Bill Nolan helped get me started on the writing career that I cherish today. (And incidentally, if you want to extend "good luck" to some aspiring young writer, don't just say, "Break a leg"; help them *do* it!) Grateful I was then, and grateful I remain for Bill's kindness, his generosity and his ongoing encouragement. Reading *Ships in the Night* likewise fills me with a deep appreciation: for the places Bill's words have taken me, the lives and adventures we've shared, the insights I have gained…and the questions that remain.

—Paul McComas
Evanston, IL

AUTHOR'S INTRODUCTION

OF MY MANY VOLUMES OF COLLECTED SHORT FICTION, *Ships in the Night* pleases me most. It is unique, my first collection to be published without regard to genre considerations. Up to now, publishers have insisted on placing my work within well-defined areas. I have been able to sell all-science-fiction collections, all-horror collections, and all-crime collections, but *Ships in the Night* is my first multiple-genre collection. Here my readers will encounter a Western story, a boxing story, a motor racing story, an aviation story, a time travel story. And more!

Today, particularly in North America, readers and critics are quick to attach a label to any writer who seems to fit a recognized genre. Stephen King is forever pegged as a horror writer, despite the fact that he has also written jazz tales, crime stories, psychological dramas, and nostalgic fantasy. Max Brand is strictly considered a Western novelist, although he wrote in a wide variety of other fields, including the iconic *Dr. Kildare* medical series. Ray Bradbury has, for many years, been bannered on paperbacks as "The World's Greatest Living Science Fiction Writer," when – in truth – beyond *Fahrenheit 451* and *The Martian Chronicles*, he has written hundreds of tales having nothing to do with future worlds or rocket ships.

I could cite several more well-known writers who have suffered from labeling. Most critics and many readers feel uneasy in dealing with a multi-genre talent. Such an individual makes them nervous; they can't fit him or her into a comfortable niche. The result: an inadequate label is arbitrarily applied. And once an incomplete label is attached to a writer, it is extremely difficult for the creator to transcend.

I have always resisted labeling with regard to my work. Because of *Logan's Run* and its sequels, I have been declared a science fiction writer. Because of my hard-boiled detective novels, I have been declared a mystery writer. Because of my dark shock-fiction tales, I have been declared a horror writer.

In truth, over the years, I have worked in a dozen different fields. I've written pieces about the world of showbiz, medical pamphlets on eye care, biographies, verse, essays, reviews, and a mass of scripts for films and television. I've written for radio, for the Internet, and for the stage. My works have been printed in an eclectic cross-cultural mix of publications from comic books to literary journals. Therefore, no single label can possibly describe my work as a writer.

Which brings us back to *Ships in the Night*. The ten stories in this collection were originally printed over a thirty-five-year span, from 1957 into 1992, and (with the exception of the title story) are presented here in the order in which they first appeared. They have never been gathered together as a collection, and three of them have never seen print in book format.

Over past decades, I have suffered intense frustration because – until now – I could never convince a publisher to put these tales together in a single, non-genre volume. Happily, thanks to Capra Press, my frustration has ended.

Here are ten of my favorite literary children. Printed *without* a label. At last.

—WILLIAM F. NOLAN
West Hills, California

I BEGIN THIS COLLECTION with "Ships in the Night" because it most closely mirrors my past; what you will read here is truth presented as fiction.

I *did* grow up in Kansas City in a house at 3337 Forest Avenue (where JoAnn McKee lived across the street). I did attend the Isis theater. I did read *Captain America* comics, was lousy at sports, and in high school never kissed a girl. I *did* own a bicycle called the Green Bullet, loved Western movies, and worked in a box factory with unfortunate results. My family's first car *was* an Auburn, and we did drive out from Missouri to California over Route 66 in a '36 Dodge. I *was* taught only by nuns through high school. (The Church almost crippled me for life; I barely escaped its pernicious hold. And my mother – a good, devout, hard-working woman – was misled and betrayed by Holy Mother

Church. As a result, I'm more than an ex-Catholic; I'm an ardent anti-Catholic.)

I was rejected for military service after World War II because of my flat feet, took all the trips mentioned here, was in a plane that lost an engine over Greenland, and had my own art studio in San Diego's Spanish Village. All true. All part of my life before 1970, when I married writer Cameron Nolan. (We'd met more than ten years earlier, at Richard and Ruth Matheson's home. Because I am still loyal to my beloved L.C. Smith-Corona Super-Speed manual typewriter – I've been working on it since the 1950s – Cam is the one who's computer-keyboarding the words you're reading here.)

However, since this story is fiction, not everything I've written about actually happened to me. I didn't almost get hit by a Chevy van; I wasn't abandoned in Mexico by gays; my father did not die at home in San Diego, but years later at a hospital in Burbank (in the San Fernando Valley of Los Angeles County). I have no cousin in New York (that I'm aware of, anyway), and I *did* write a best-selling book: *Logan's Run*.

But "Ships in the Night" is as close to straight autobiography as I could make it. For better or worse, I am Harvey.

His world is mine.

SHIPS IN THE NIGHT

HARVEY GOT THE IDEA when he was crossing Hollywood Boulevard earlier that evening and a drunk swerved around the corner from Highland, hellbent, in a Chevy van. Harvey had leaped back, with the drunk's front bumper brushing his right trouser leg. There was a small spot of grease near his knee where the bumper had scraped the cloth.

"That son of a bitch ought to be arrested!" declared a woman just behind Harvey. "They should haul in that god-damn bastard and throw the key away."

Harvey blinked at her, saying nothing. He hated to hear a woman swear, and her words disturbed him almost as much as the drunk's van. She was an attractive woman in her mid-forties, and now she was smiling at him. Maybe she was a prostitute; there were a lot of them in Hollywood.

Harvey turned his back on her and walked rapidly away.

By the time he reached his hotel on Sunset, he had worked out the idea. He thought: I'll never see that drunk again, or that woman either. They are gone. Ships in the night. That's all most people are; even the ones you work with, make friends with or go to school with. Some of them stay in sight longer, and a few are with you for many years, but eventually they all drift into the darkness and you're left alone. Even your parents die, as Harvey's had died. If you get married you fight with your wife, get a divorce, and never see each other again. Or your wife dies. Or else you never get married in the first place, as Harvey had never married.

He walked into the lobby, past the dying potted plant, excited with this idea of his. All the way up the stairs he was outlining his approach, mentally cataloguing various sections. He could envision the whole thing, page after page of it, and it really excited him inside. He felt *powerful* – to be able to put this thing together the way he planned. It was really going to be something.

Inside the apartment, he didn't take off his coat, just sat down at the small, square kitchen table with a pad of paper and a Bic ballpoint and began writing, fast as he could, beginning with the names of all the girls he'd ever known. He decided that he would start with girls he'd known in Kansas City as a child. The first one he could think of was JoAnn McKee, who lived across the street and who used to invite him to her birthday parties. Harvey remembered being very uncomfortable at these parties, and there was a photo, in his mother's album, of Harvey standing off to the side looking lost and unhappy, at one of JoAnn McKee's parties.

He broke the list into GIRLS and WOMEN. Girls were the ones up to their twenties. He thought of doing a separate listing for GIRLFRIENDS, but that would be depressing because the list would be so short. He'd never been successful with girls, had never learned to dance, and had gone all through high school into the last half of his senior year without going on a single date. Then he'd gone out, finally, with Betty Brown, roller skating and to the movies, but he'd never kissed her. He had *wanted* to kiss her. He thought of it a lot. He'd also thought of touching her breasts through those soft pink sweaters she always wore, but he hadn't dared try. In confession, to Father Flaherty, he'd confessed these thoughts as "impure." They weren't. They were just normal. But he was a Catholic in those days, a strict one, and Catholic boys didn't think about sex. Not without committing a sin, that is.

He hated Holy Mother Church for what it had done to him. He'd gone to a Catholic grade school for seven years, then into four years of Catholic high school – all under the domination of black-robed nuns. Some of the nuns were okay, but many were dour, warped, frustrated women who poured their emotional sickness into vulnerable young minds.

He thought about his parents – both Catholics. His father had been divorced before he married Harvey's mom and didn't go to Mass anymore. Later, his mother started going to Mass again, but she had to promise God, through a priest, that she would no longer have sexual relations with Harvey's father – in order to receive the sacraments. That was the kind of perversion generated by Holy Mother Church.

Mom *did* reject the Church in her final years, thought Harvey, and she died without a priest. Which showed a lot of courage. She'd been a good woman, but the Church betrayed her and destroyed her marriage.

And me with it, thought Harvey, it destroyed me too, laying on feelings of guilt and self-shame, assaulting my senses with constant warnings of fire and brimstone and eternal damnation. Anti-human, anti-life, that's what the Church was and is, a crippler and a destroyer. The true miracle of the Church, thought Harvey, is that I escaped it. But not without scars. There are many good people in the Church, but the base, the *core*, is essentially perverted. Harvey knew that it had ruined his life in many ways, and that he was, forever, a sexual cripple because of Holy Mother Church. He *should* have touched Betty Brown's breasts. He damn well should have!

He kept working, adding new lists. It got dark outside, a slow-gathering grayness that turned into night – and suddenly Harvey couldn't see to write. Sighing, he snapped on the kitchen light. By then he'd started putting down the names of men as well as women, of clerks and store workers and bosses and friends. FRIENDS was a separate listing and disappointed Harvey since there were so few names to write down. I'm too introverted, he told himself, not outgoing enough to make a lot of friends. I could never tell a joke.

Harvey could feel tiny pearls of sweat on his upper lip and forehead as he concentrated. He was now putting down the names of all the authors he had read, the ones who had really touched his life, as so many had. And he was trying to pinpoint the era of each book, when he had read it, what year, and this was difficult. He'd have to look at copyright dates, but that could come later. Just get the titles down now, he told himself.

Harvey got up stiffly from the table thinking, you're sixty and that's the entry to old age. He hated being sixty; it was a cheat. He hadn't done enough living to be sixty.

He walked into the bedroom (full of books, as the whole apartment was full of them) and leaned over the metal filing cabinet. All of his personal papers were here, along with his diaries and address books. Thank God he'd kept all these address books over the years because they were full of names he'd completely forgotten. Bits of the mosaic he needed.

Scooping up all the papers, Harvey took them to the kitchen table and dumped everything there, pushing aside the salt and pepper shakers and the toaster; he needed space for this job.

He looked at the index material first. He'd made an index of all his books, about five thousand titles, and an index of his LPs and of his home-recorded tapes and cassettes. He even found an old index, written in pencil on faded yellow paper, of his 78-rpm records, which had long since been given away or abandoned as he moved. But this index was fine to have now; he could list the special records that had affected him, such as *Old Buttermilk Sky* – which reminded him of a Christmas party in 1940, before the war, when a friend of his mother had brought her twelve-year-old daughter. *Old Buttermilk Sky* had been playing on the phonograph. The girl had stunned his shy boy's heart with her beauty. So much older than her years. Like a young goddess. What was her name? He would need it for the list. He'd never seen her again after that night, but her name surely must be in one of the diaries. He was certain he could find it.

Harvey felt a stab of hunger, annoying him, disrupting his concentration. He'd have to eat something. Anything would do, just to quiet his stomach. He opened the small chipped fridge and got out some sliced cheese. Then he tore off a hunk of French bread, smearing it with yellow mustard. He stuffed the food into his mouth, gulping at a can of 7-Up, and resenting the time he was losing. He didn't want to break the rhythm of this thing; it was vast, complicated, vital.

Harvey had read a book on the brain, and he knew that it could store six hundred memories per second for seventy-five years: which meant that every moment of his life was inside his head, that everything he'd ever seen, heard, or done was in there....

He marked PLACES LIVED at the top of a page. The first place he'd lived, through his teen years, was in the small family home on Forest Avenue in Kansas City. Carefully, he wrote the words KANSAS CITY.

For Harvey, Kansas City meant the earth-damp, shaded passageway between two garages behind his house, leading to Don's place (his one boyhood pal); it meant climbing the pear tree in tight new birthday shoes to his special secret treehouse; it meant long afternoons in the back driveway, building his own tiny roads, pushing the gray-white gravel into mounds, then running toy cars down these new highways while the other neighborhood kids played baseball. (He had an eye problem, and was never good at sports.) Kansas City meant sledding in winter, going into the basement for his Red Racer and cleaning rust and cobwebs off the runners; it meant rushing up the hill from Forest to Troost to buy the latest issue of *Captain America* from the drugstore rack and inhaling the rich, inky odor of the 10-cent comic as he read it, mesmerized, walking home; it meant sitting on the porch swing at night counting fireflies and listening to the radio which glowed warmly through the dark, screened window, and sipping cold lemonade and feeling he'd be there, safe with Mom and Dad, forever.

Harvey remembered the horse-drawn ice wagon and the cake of melting crystal slung over the iceman's gunny-sacked shoulder, held there by silver pincers, and the way the iceman brought the smells of canvas and wet leather into the kitchen. He remembered the old coal-burning furnace in the basement, that ravenous contraption with its slotted-iron door, and the arrival of the coal truck in winter, grinding along the snow-packed driveway to disgorge its tumble of glittery black coal down the racketing tin chute into the basement. And he remembered penny candy in a giant glass bowl on the marble soda fountain in Rae's Drugstore, and the heady freedom of his bicycle (the Green Bullet!), waiting to take him to magic places far beyond Forest Avenue....

He had been away from Kansas City for more than two decades when he was passing through Missouri on the train and suddenly decided to visit his old neighborhood. A mistake, for sure. He'd rented a car in downtown K.C. and had driven toward his home street. So much had changed! The big, wooden-covered roller rink in Gillham Plaza, where he'd skated with Betty, was now a warehouse. The whole area was in decline. The red-brick storefronts were chipped and blackened, their windows fogged with dust. Troost was a ghost street; the Isis Theater, where he'd watched Errol Flynn and Gary Cooper for a dime at Saturday Matinees, was closed and boarded over. The Bluebird Cafeteria was gone (meals for a quarter!) – and at the bottom of the hill at 33rd, a vacant, weedy lot led to Forest Avenue.

Harvey had walked to his old house, halfway down the block, over the cracked, root-swollen sidewalk, past sagging Victorian structures, to 3337 Forest. He stared at the small, paint-blistered one story frame house, weathered and raw looking in the sharp white glare of the summer sun. The porch was rotted, with broken posts and warped wooden steps; the attic window was shattered, the roof in sorry disrepair, the gravel driveway rutted and unkempt, the front yard an overgrown weed patch.

People and houses – they get old.

Harvey drew in a breath. Damn! He'd never get this job done if he didn't *concentrate*. No more mental wandering. Just names, places, dates – hard facts on paper. That was the only way to get it all down.

Quickly, then, he scrawled JOBS as a heading, then, in rapid succession, with a heading for each page, he jotted down SCHOOLS, BOYHOOD IDOLS, FAMILY ASSOCIATES, CITIES VISITED, ENEMIES MADE. He began to fill in these sections, working from his papers, reaching deep into the vaults of memory to compile the lists.

Under CITIES VISITED, as he wrote "Washington, D.C.," he remembered how cold he'd been walking down Capitol Hill from the Library of Congress with the wind cutting at his face. The assault was so fierce he had to turn around and walk backwards down the hill to escape the force of that terrible wind. He'd been alone in the city, as he'd been alone in so many cities, and he had nowhere special to go after his research work, so he went back to his hotel for a hot bath.

Now Harvey was thinking of other cold cities he'd known. His own home town in winter, of St. Louis, and the cold at night along the river when he'd taken a sight-seeing tour, of Detroit and Toledo, two iron-cold cities he had hated. New York and Chicago had been cold, too, but he hadn't minded it so much in those cities; he actually enjoyed their snow after the dulling, perpetual heat of California where he'd lived since leaving Missouri.

As a free-lance writer, trying to survive from book to book (he'd never had a best-seller), Harvey had visited many cities for research purposes. There was New Orleans, with its muddy-brown sweep of Mississippi, where the rain had come down in a blinding rush, a Niagara of water. The rain made him think of lightning, and of the weird, dream-like needling-down of the long, jagged Frankenstein bolts at the horizon's edge in New Mexico, when he'd been on a train heading for Albuquerque, and the train had stopped due to an electrical storm, and he'd pressed his face to the

43

cool glass of the window, dreaming of what it might be to leave the Earth forever and live up there with the lightning, away from bills and people and problems.

I'm drifting again, Harvey told himself sharply. I must try to keep from drifting, but it isn't easy. Thoughts overlapped and blended; images came unbidden, rushing into his head....

There was Mexico, and the painting trip he'd taken with a couple of artist friends he'd met in San Diego. They told him they wanted to paint in Mexico and why not come with them? So the three had driven down the length of coast highway in an old dented Ford. Harvey had gone barefoot in the sun and had burned the skin off his feet so badly he couldn't wear shoes for a week. The blisters had been as large as quarters.

The three of them had driven all the way downcoast, to where the paved highway suddenly ended – and on the way back the worn gear in the rear axle had sheared and they were forced to tow the car across the border at night over a dry river bed, because in Mexico you couldn't tow a car back into the States. At least that's what his friend had told him.

Mexico... There was San Felipe, a tiny strip of village hugging the edge of the Gulf which looked untouched by civilization until you got closer and saw the big 7-Up and Coca-Cola signs. That had been a bizarre trip. Harvey and his two artist friends, leaving Los Angeles after dark and driving all night. They'd stopped about 10 a.m. at some little, dried-up desert town (What was the town's name? It should go on the list.) and rented rooms on the top floor of an ancient, paint-flaked wooden hotel. That was when one of the artists came into Harvey's room and put his hand on Harvey's leg. It was a real shock, and Harvey told him to get the hell out of his room and the guy left.

After that, the two artists abandoned him there at the hotel and he had to hitch a ride back to the border in a flatbed truck. That had been Harvey's only experience with homosexuals.

Harvey wondered if he should use a separate page headed TRIP TO EUROPE. He decided this was a good idea, and under this new heading he began listing all the cities he'd seen in that quick week he'd flown to Europe and back. The plane was one of the last of the piston engine aircraft and was ready for retirement. They had, in fact, lost an engine over Greenland and had to land in a remote spot called Sondre Stromfourd (the spelling was wrong, he knew, but he could check it later in the world atlas). Odd place. Daylight all the time. They had to stay there for twenty-four hours until a new engine was installed, and it never got dark. A kind of lunar landscape, unreal and barren. Then there was Copenhagen, where he'd spent the night beyond town, in some castle where Hamlet was supposed to have lived – or was it Richard the Third? Some big shot. (That's what his Mom called people who had money or were famous; Harvey's family was strictly working class. He'd never be a big shot.)

Monte Carlo looked like a candy city from the sky, bright and multicolored, as they swung along the Mediterranean coast toward Nice. After a night on the Blue

Train, he had arrived in Paris, its streets and buildings ablaze under the sun, dazzling as diamonds.

There had been a brief stop in Canada on the way over, and he recalled the dark, stained-green look of the hills – and the flies at the airport in Ontario.

The flies made Harvey think of the Lake of the Ozarks, and the fishing trips he'd taken with Dad each summer. His father loved trolling the lake, while Harvey rowed (he didn't like fishing; hooking worms bothered him a lot). He could still hear the buzzing of the flies around his head when he tried to eat watermelon out on the lake while his father fished the deep hollows. When you move away from Missouri, to California, you forget the flies, Harvey thought. Every summer there were millions of them in Missouri, but you just brushed them away. He was thinking of the flies now for the first time in years.

The lake had been an immense sheet of black glass at night on those long-ago fishing trips, with the moon trailing over it softly, not disturbing the surface at all. You could hear the motorboats, way off in night distance, making for their home docks, buzzing like the flies.…

Harvey was mind-drifting again, and it angered him. Names. Just the names. Later he could fill in some descriptive prose, impressions and memories, but names were the important thing now.

He jotted down "Curwood" under FAVORITE AUTHORS, with *Kazan* in parenthesis – to remind him of this book in particular. James Oliver Curwood's *Kazan*. Half dog, half wolf. He found the novel deep in basement darkness – the first adult book he'd ever owned. He remembered reading it while flat on his back in the rusted iron bed of his red wagon outside the A&P store on Troost. He was supposed to be waiting for ladies to hire him (for 10 cents a trip) to pull their groceries home in his wagon. But he forgot all about ladies and groceries and shiny dimes when he was reading *Kazan*, got lost in the pages and moved only when it started to rain and the drops began leaving little stains, like blisters, on the green cloth binding.

Rain reminded Harvey of his Uncle Frank, because it had been raining in the cemetery in Kansas City when they had buried him – and way over the hill, out of sight, someone played taps on an army bugle. Harvey's mother had cried a lot. Frank was her favorite brother and had a special place in her heart. That bugle was the saddest sound Harvey had ever heard, and when the last long metallic note faded to silence his Uncle Frank was in the ground and they were pulling up the long straps that had been used to lower the coffin. And it kept raining, thinner now, a misting kind of rain like smoke on the hill....

Harvey wondered what it would be like to have children, and what your children would think when they saw you put in the ground? Would they be brave, like Uncle Frank's children – or would they go to pieces the way Harvey had done when his father was dying in the front room of the house in San Diego and the priest was giving the Last Sacraments and Harvey was in the kitchen, by the stove, shaking wildly, like a man in front of a firing squad?

Harvey thought of all the children he had known and

began writing their names on the page headed CHILDREN
I HAVE KNOWN, and as he wrote he thought that kids
were fine in short doses, were fun to play with for a little
while, but that they made him quite nervous after about fifteen minutes. It was a good thing he'd never had children.
Once, in his Catholic years, at a Mass in Burbank, he'd seen
a married couple come in with a whole flock of kids. The
mother went into the pew first, then all these children followed her in, herded by their father who took his weary
place at the end of the pew, kneeling there with a harried
expression. The entire pew was filled, just with the children
of this one couple. Harvey had watched them with a kind
of numb shock as the kids plucked at one another, whispered, grinned over their shoulders, pulled hair, tore up
donation envelopes – while the mother read her prayer
book and the father fired stern, withering glances out along
the pew like shots from a rifle. He finally shoulder-punched
one of the boys and this temporarily silenced the others.

One of Harvey's high school friends sired eleven children, became an alcoholic, and left his family to live alone
in a boathouse on Lake Lotawana. Claimed he had never
wanted to be a father.

Harvey turned his attention to the sheet marked JOBS.
He made a list of twenty jobs held before he became a
writer. As a boy, he had delivered the *Saturday Evening Post*
door to door, but he was a poor salesman and ended up
with just three customers. He'd been a cigar store clerk (but
had never smoked), a theater usher (they don't have them
anymore, he realized, not in movie houses), a stock room

helper, and a warehouse worker. He remembered the sharp smell of fresh-cut paper at the mill in Kansas City, and the big machine that fed out the cut sections, like slices of bread, which had to be stacked neatly on rolling carts. Harvey had piled his feeder stack at a crooked angle one afternoon and the whole cart turned over, spilling boxes halfway across the floor. It was the first time the shop foreman had been forced to shut down the paper machine during working hours, and Harvey had been deeply depressed over having been the cause of the shutdown. On his break that day, lying on a high stack of cardboard boxes, he had brooded about his basic incompetence. The other workers had shunned him; no one else in the shop had ever caused the machine to stop. Just one more proof that he didn't fit it, didn't function well in general society.

He'd been a parking lot attendant without being able to drive (when he finally learned he almost wrecked the family car), and he lasted just one day in downtown K.C. as a tie salesman.

He counted himself lucky that he was never in the service. He knew he'd have made a terrible soldier. After the war with Hitler had ended, Harvey had been called to Fort Leavenworth, in Kansas, for an army exam. He had feared being drafted. He could still feel the hard baked-leather seat of the bus pressing into his back and the strain on his kidneys, riding with this shouting group of teenagers out to the Fort for their physicals. They turned out to be healthy fellows, and were taken into the service, and only Harvey was rejected. Fallen arches. Flat feet. He remembered riding back alone in the empty bus to K.C. feeling that he had "lucky feet." They had kept him out of the army.

The bus made Harvey turn his thoughts toward cars, the automobiles that had affected his life, and he quickly headed a sheet with CARS IN MY LIFE. The first one he could remember was a long green Auburn his father had been so proud of, with huge headlamps and mohair upholstery. It was replaced by the car Harvey learned to drive when he was eighteen, a black 1936 Dodge with a floor shift. Fritz McGrath, a friend from high school, had taught Harvey to drive in that old Dodge, risking death on the gravel back-country roads outside K.C. when Harvey had mistaken the gas pedal for the brake and had driven them over a bridge and into a ditch. The black Dodge had borne Harvey's family to California, like a faithful horse, crossing the country on Route 66. And it had been sold in San Diego for what they'd originally paid for it: $200. Next, they got an Oldsmobile with a Hydromatic shift that Harvey's Aunt Grace had sold them, but the Olds had expired in San Francisco, and Harvey had bought a new cream-colored Ford sedan with his paycheck from the aircraft plant where he worked as a parts inspector.

The intrusive blare of a TV set in the next apartment made Harvey quit thinking about cars. He heard sounds that were wonderfully familiar: hoofbeats, shouts, gunshots, the yipping cries of wild Indians – and he thought of *Stagecoach* and *Shane* and *My Darling Clementine* and *High Noon* and *The Big Country* – and of Gary Cooper as Bill Hickok in *The Plainsman*, which Harvey had seen at the age of seven and had never forgotten. Ah, how he loved Westerns!

In an earlier time, thought Harvey, I might have been a cowboy, riding alone, working in the wilds, with no rules to tie me down. A free way to live.

Should he list all the movies he'd seen up to now? Not just Westerns, but all the others? He went every week. Sometimes, he saw two films the same day; once, alone in Times Square, he'd seen four movies in an afternoon. The total must be into the thousands! He couldn't remember all the titles. Impossible. He settled for listing BEST LOVED MOVIES, and worked on this list for the next hour.

The lists grew longer as the night hours drifted past. Harvey carefully consulted each page of his diaries and address books and personal papers. He wrote until his back ached, his neck cramped, until his eyes were blurring the words. But he didn't stop.

He felt the power. If he concentrated, focused in, remembered it all, got it all down, he could hold life here in this room, halting the process of aging and decay. He felt this glowing power, almost mystical, in his fingers. Don't question it, Harvey told himself, just go with it....

He listed the names of all the artists in San Diego's Spanish Village, where he'd once had a studio, and he listed the names of the people who had worked with him at Convair and at the Department of Employment in Inglewood – and he wrote down the names of all the people he knew in the credit department of Blake, Moffit and Towne Paper Company in downtown Los Angeles, headed by the name of the miserable man who'd been his boss there. He put down the names of all the great movie stars he'd loved, and of all his family members from a scrapbook of photos his mother had given him, then of people his father had known…and of all the dead people he could think of and he listed the items in his apartment and the furniture they'd had in Kansas City….

A pale dawn was tinting the sky outside the hotel window when Harvey crawled, exhausted, into bed, his fingers stiff and numbed and his head throbbing from pressure.

He lay staring at the ceiling, unsatisfied. It wasn't complete. There were more lists to be made, but not here, not in Hollywood. New York! That was where he'd go – to the Big Apple. He had a cousin there who ran a deli; Harvey could go to work for him. He thought of all the glittering shops along Fifth Avenue. Full of items to list. Tons of items. Countless numbers of them.

There was so *much* he could do in New York.

I'M GRATIFIED TO REPORT that this story was selected (in the U.K.) for *Best Motor Racing Stories* and appeared in three U.S. textbooks, notably in *A Guidebook to Better Reading*. It is authentic to the smallest detail, a totally accurate reflection of sports car competition during the 1950s.

When "The Ragged Edge" was written, I was deeply involved in the world of fast cars. I owned (and competed in) a British Austin-Healey Le Mans 100-M ("M" for "modified"), the same model that had been tested in motorized battle during the Le Mans twenty-four-hour race in France. I won a trophy driving the Healey at the Hour-Glass Circuit near San Diego, and staged impromptu (and illegal) sports car races at an abandoned housing tract in the San Fernando Valley. I wrote for all the competition magazines, knew all the top sports car drivers, and attended races around the world, from Sebring to Nassau to Monte Carlo.

Eventually, I produced eight books dealing with this sport.

As a columnist for *Badge Bar Journal*, I covered every California event from Riverside to Pebble Beach. Ah…Pebble Beach. I never raced there, but I knew this deadly, twisting, tree-lined course quite well indeed. I saw ace driver Ernie McAfee crash and die there, and I watched Phil Hill (the first American to become a Formula One World Champion) challenge an all-star field to achieve a well-earned victory at this circuit.

"The Ragged Edge," which is set at Pebble Beach, has a factual basis. It was inspired by the tenacious, real-life driving of one William Eschrich, a Burbank doctor who – accompanied by his two teenaged sons – competed at every major West Coast event.

The good doctor, with his swift "Eschrich Special," was always in solid contention, but he never managed to finish a race. Something always failed on his car. As a writer, I asked myself: What might happen if his Special didn't break down before reaching the checkered flag?

This story, first printed in 1957, supplies the answer.

THE RAGGED EDGE

As usual, Linda had remembered to have the thermos refilled at the last coffee stop just before dawn, and now Robert March held the steaming metal cup in his two hands, grateful for the steady warmth in the early morning. A clouded sun was just breaking over the tall trees fringing the track, and March inhaled the rich, moist scent of pine, carried to him by the chill ocean wind off the Pacific.

"At least we're good and early," he said to his wife.

Linda March smiled. She was a small-boned delicate woman with soft brown hair combed loosely back from a high forehead. "I knew we would be," she said.

March thought of his first race here at Pebble Beach last year, when they had arrived late at the track, and he had almost failed to run. This weekend would be different.

This weekend, he vowed, must be different.

Ahead of him, across the uneven ground, the long

wooden inspection tables were already up, and girls in blue coveralls had arranged themselves in canvas chairs behind their charts and papers. Standing by the open door of the Chrysler, March sipped his coffee and watched the low-slung sports cars being pushed into line for technical inspection. His own machine, the March Special, was third behind a white Jaguar coupe.

"I'd better get on over there," March said, handing Linda his empty cup. "Keep the coffee hot."

"Tell Randy to put on his sweater," Linda instructed him, reaching into the Chrysler's rear seat for the garment. "It's windy this morning."

As March walked toward the inspection grid, he thought about the Special, about what the race tomorrow really meant to him. He thought of Bakersfield and the broken fuel pump in the fourth lap, of Santa Barbara and the wheel he'd lost on the hairpin, of Torrey Pines and the sudden, terrible dip of the pressure needle, telling him that his oil was gone; he thought of the long, uphill turn at Willow Springs, when the rear axle had broken and he'd spun out. And he thought, finally of the big one last year, right here at Pebble Beach, when he'd been doing fine, coming up steadily through the pack, and the transmission had blown. Always something. *Something.*

You're a doctor, March told himself, a family man of forty with a fine wife and two nearly-grown sons. You don't belong in sports car racing and you know it. You're in it because you wanted to prove that you could take a car you'd built yourself and finish with the best of them. Well, you've tried; for a year now you've tried, and you've failed. You haven't finished one race, not one. So, why go on playing the fool?

"Hi, Dad!" The voices of his twin sons, Glenn and Randy, cut into his thoughts.

"Hi, boys," he grinned. "We're up next, aren't we?"

"Yeah. Give us a hand, Dad."

March tossed Randy's sweater into the cockpit and helped his two sixteen-year-old sons push the big blue Special into the slot vacated by the Jag.

March handed the check-off sheet to inspector Bill Greer. "Think you'll blow off all the competition tomorrow, Doc?" asked the beefy little man, beginning his methodical safety check. He chuckled softly.

"Don't worry about Dad, Mr. Greer," Randy said stiffly. "Just let the other drivers do the worrying."

March could see that Randy was upset.

How do you feel, wondered Robert March, when you've got a father who never finishes? The boys had helped him put the Special together, worked with him on every detail, pitching in after school and on weekends to get the car ready. And then – eleven races and he'd never crossed the finish line. The constant ribbing from the other drivers had been hard to take, and he could see that Randy and Glenn were badly shaken by each new disaster. For them, the scorn and barbed humor cut deep.

Then why go on? Even Linda, who understood him completely, was beginning to worry. She knew the risks he took out there on the track, and accepted them calmly because that was her nature, but even Linda was concerned now over the boys. She had watched them become nervous and unhappy as the months went by, as the failures mounted, and she was worried.

All right, then, tomorrow would be the last one, the last time he'd race the Special. After tomorrow, if he couldn't finish with the car, he would quit for good. He'd give himself and the Special one more chance.

"Okay, Doc," said Bill Greer, checking off the last item on the sheet, "take 'er away."

Inside the cockpit, March jabbed the starter button and the big modified Mercury engine boomed fiercely into life under the long hood.

"She sounds sweet," Randy said, as they rolled toward the pits. "Real sweet."

Saturday practice was scheduled to begin immediately after the noon drivers' meeting, and already the crowds were pressing in, filling the grandstands along the main straight, posting themselves behind the sloping wooden snowfencing which lined the entire course, settling down with blankets and food and programs, waiting to see their favorite drivers and cars bullet over the treacherous 2.1 mile Pebble Beach circuit.

March was glad that the entire afternoon had been given over to practice. Here was the most beautiful and the most dangerous circuit on the West Coast, slightly over two miles of narrow blacktop, twisting through thick forest above exclusive Del Monte Lodge, with a deadly proportion of uphill and downhill turns. The massed trunks of pine and cypress waited along every straight and curve, ready to crush car and driver. A serious mistake here could well prove fatal. Practice, at Pebble Beach, was very necessary.

"Clock my last three laps," March told his wife, as he climbed into the cockpit. "Up to then I'll just be feeling out the circuit."

"Take it easy, hon," she warned him. "I've only got one of you." He was pulling on the white crash helmet when Lou Coppard walked over to the Special. Tall and relaxed with the lean face of a wolfhound, Coppard had been openly contemptuous of March from the beginning. He never missed an opportunity to needle him about the Special.

"How's the patient, Doc?" he asked, grinning crookedly.

"She'll live," March said, his voice edged and cold.

"I should have remembered to bring flowers."

"Save 'em, Lou. Maybe you'll need 'em yourself."

"How long do you figure she'll stay pasted together out there, Doc?" Coppard asked, the grin still fixed on his lean face.

"Long enough," March replied, and decided against adding more. Don't let him get at you today, he told himself. Tomorrow, out on the track, maybe you can take him and settle the score.

The starter gave the signal to move and Coppard returned to his car. March eased the big Special through the pit gate and onto the starting grid.

As he was flagged away he forced himself to think only of the track, of how soon he needed to downshift for the uphill hairpin, of his best line through the fast corners, of when he needed to use the brakes and when he didn't.

He had a lot to learn before tomorrow.

In the late evening dusk Robert March walked back to the hotel, smoking, moving leisurely over the darkening streets, allowing himself to be caught up in that rare atmosphere characterizing such a weekend. Tonight, the small towns along the length of California's Monterey Peninsula were transformed, magically charged with a festive pre-race electricity. In dozens of shop windows tall posters boldly announced: PEBBLE BEACH SPORTS CAR ROAD RACES. Neoned NO VACANCY signs glowed above every roadside motel and the streets were filled with the ragged thunder of sports cars, a veritable sea of out-of-towners gunning their swift machines through traffic, shattering the cool night air with their loud exhausts.

Practice had gone well at least. The Special had performed perfectly throughout the entire session; she seemed ready for her biggest try. March had lapped within a second or two of some of the hottest pilots, proving the Special had the juice if she'd only hold.

She'll hold, March told himself, because this is her last chance; tomorrow she's *got* to hold.

Sunday morning dawned hot and clear at the track, with no hint of the rain that had been threatening all week. The sun rode a cloudless blue sky, filtering through the trees in checkered patches of light and shade.

Robert March had spent the early part of the day on the winding cliff roads above the Pacific, relaxing with Linda in the cool breeze from the ocean.

He told her of the decision he'd made.

"If I don't finish today, I'm quitting, Linda. Things can't go on this way."

"Are you sure, Bob? Is it what you really want?"

"Yes, I'm sure. You can't go on beating your head against a stone wall and expect the wall to give. This is my last try."

She had looked at him silently for a long moment, then taken his hand firmly in hers. "Whatever you really want is what I want too. I won't worry, no matter what you decide, I promise. Just remember that, darling."

They arrived at the track after the Cypress Point Race had been run.

March left Linda with Randy and Glenn in the pit and walked over to have a look at Jeffry Moore's Monza Ferrari. Moore was a nice guy, and a hell of a driver. Whenever he was out there with the Ferrari the competition had something to worry about.

The car was undergoing wheelwork. The low, scooped snout of the fierce Italian car almost touched the ground, the sweeping lines of the compact body proclaiming sheer speed. Of course the Monza had been geared down for Pebble, but it would be reaching 130 on the back straight, and that was moving. However, Moore would have to reckon with Fischer's powerful D-type Jaguar and Wyndham's Maserati. A furious three-way battle to the checkered flag was in prospect.

"Going to ride her all the way home today, Doc?" asked a familiar voice, and March turned to face Jeffry Moore, resplendent in immaculate white coveralls. Like most of the aces, Moore wore his fame with a casual indifference, but behind the easy smile, behind the friendly squint of the narrow gray eyes, March was aware of the nervous pulse of electricity which only the track could completely remove. Only on the track, screaming down a long straight or fighting a tight curve, could a man like Moore wholly become himself.

"I'm going to try to keep you boys in sight," March replied. "I figure the Special is as ready as she'll ever be."

"That's just it, Doc," said Moore, his tone serious. "We all give you the business about the Special, but I, for one, hate to see a guy knock himself out for nothing. The car hasn't got it. She's full of bugs and bad luck, and you know it. We all know it. If you want to race then get into a car that will give you an even break. Right now Ray Boucher has one of his Ferraris up for sale. You could handle her, Doc."

"Thanks, Jeff, but I've got other plans."

"Okay. Hope she holds for you today."

"Yeah," said March. "I hope so too."

The furnace-heat of the sun seemed focused on the starting grid as the glittering line of cars rolled slowly into position for the last race of the day. This was the main event, the one the crowds had been waiting for. In just a few breathless moments the green flag would drop on thirty-two of the world's fastest sports cars, on one and a half hours of all-out driving for the coveted Del Monte trophy.

From his assigned position in the fourth row, next to a modified Healey 100S, Robert March could feel the tension, a thing alive, growing around him.

"You stick with 'er, Dad," Randy was saying. He patted the lean aluminum shell of the Merc-powered Special. "She'll go all the way for you this time, I *know* she will."

"You'd better get on back with Linda and Glenn," March said, as the clear-grid order crackled over the high black cluster of loudspeakers. They shook hands and Randy stepped away.

So, here we are, thought Robert March, flexing and unflexing his gloved hands on the spidery racing wheel. This is the last one, the one that really counts. He adjusted his goggles against the raw glare of sun on polished metal and waited.

A gradual silence fell upon the crowds in the grandstand and along the length of wooden snowfence fronting start-finish. Tensely they waited for starter Al Tucker to begin his final checkrun down the line of cars.

The sun lay on March's neck and shoulders, a hot, blazing weight, pressing him deeper into the bucket seat. Already the sweat had soaked through the back of his coveralls, and the safety belt felt like a band of steel across his hips. Damn it, Tucker, let's get the show on the road! Every second he sat there in the broiling heat, a taut spring was winding itself tighter within his body.

He thought of the men and machines around him, of Al Fischer in the incredibly fast D-Jag, of Jeff Moore's Monza

Ferrari, of Wyndham in the Maserati. What a battle these three would wage! He thought, too, of Tim Mulford's huge 4.9 Ferrari. Tim might take an early lead with the brutish car, but he would be unable to hold it on a tight course like Pebble. Chuck Quavale in the Buick-Kurtis was always a solid threat. Finally, March thought of Lou Coppard. He could see Lou's face, framed in the rear-view mirror. His black Cadillac-powered Special was two rows back, on the inside. The rest of the leadfoots could battle it out for the cup; March only wanted two things in this race. He wanted to finish – and he wanted Coppard's scalp.

He pulled his helmet strap tight and forced his full attention to Al Tucker as the little man signaled start-engines.

The sudden thunder of thirty-two finely-tuned racing engines washed over the grid, the sharp roar of the Buick-Kurtis blending with the knifing shriek of the Ferraris. Every eye was on Al Tucker as the harlequin-shirted little man fell into his jogging Indian-run down the line of poised machinery. March raised a gloved hand to let Tucker know he was ready and firing.

At the end of the line Tucker pivoted gracefully and loped back to the front row, the green flag furled and ready in his hand. He paused dramatically, back to the drivers. The engines screamed. Only seconds now.

I've been here for a century, thought Robert March, belted to a tiger, waiting. Dear God, man, will you *jump*? Tucker leaped high into the air and the green flag swirled free. The taut spring in Robert March's body uncoiled. He mashed down on the gas pedal and felt the dizzying surge of acceleration as the massive Special rocketed forward.

He saw Tim Mulford's big Ferrari rip into the first sweeping turn just ahead of Fischer's D-Jag. Moore and Wyndham went in snapping at the leaders' heels. Just ahead of March, Chuck Quavale powered his Buick-Kurtis in wide, passing two slower machines in the apex of the turn.

March was seventh coming out of turn three into the winding, uphill hairpin, and he was hanging on to Quavale. As they roared through the dog-leg bend Lou Coppard's black Cad-Special whipped into sight in his rear view mirror.

So, he wants his dice early, eh? thought March. All right, Lou, make your bid. I'm ready.

He'd planned on conserving his brakes through the beginning laps, but now he saw this was not possible if he wished to take Coppard.

They swung into the long back straight, down through turn six, and swept full-throttle past the pits and grandstand. A rough circuit, March thought, a really mean one.

They boomed past Donaldson's stalled V8-60 Special on the main straight with Coppard pressing hard, a scant two car-lengths to March's rear. On the short, twisty stretch into the hairpin, the cut-off markers jumped at them, and March braked, dumping into a lower gear for the tight corner. Coppard moved up another two feet.

The tachometer needle climbed crazily as March floored the pedal on the long back straight. The straining Merc engine shrilled under full-throttle, and the haybales, solid as stones at this speed, flashed by in a yellow-bright pattern under the sun. Behind the bales the threatening bulk of trees blurred with speed into a single dark line.

A modified Triumph had spun into the bales on turn six, and March was forced to cramp the wheel hard-right to avoid an accident. He saw Coppard slew by, barely missing the derelict car.

The pace quickened.

Coppard, driving at the peak of his form, closed to within a half car-length on the front straight, and March wondered if he could hold him through the dog-leg at this speed.

At that precise instant Coppard's right rear tire blew, with a flat crack, sharp as a rifle shot, and the black Special skidded across the width of the track, spun twice, and came to rest with the other three tires smoking.

As he entered the first sweeping bend March could see Lou Coppard, obviously unhurt, gesturing wildly to his pit crew. By the time he could get a new tire on the car March would be half a lap ahead. The dice was over.

All right, let's start saving those brakes, March told himself. You've got better than an hour left to run.

On the next lap, as he swept past the pits, he caught the chalked numeral on the blackboard that Randy held out for him. P-6. Which meant he had emerged from the dice in sixth position!

He recognized Mulford's 4.9 Ferrari in the pits; Tim, of course, had pushed too hard. That meant Fischer in the D-Jag was leading somewhere up ahead, probably followed by Moore's Ferrari and Wyndham's Maserati. He could see Quavale's Kurtis and Gene Waring in the C-Jag ahead of him as he entered the back straight. He was running sixth, behind Waring.

March felt the heat from the straining engine fire up along his legs; he inhaled the bitter-sharp scent of burned rubber and hot oil – and he thought, by God, she's holding, she's doing fine. Forty-two minutes to go.

According to Randy's pit board he was now picking up on Gene Waring at the rate of three seconds a lap.

He was still closing when Waring's car hit a patch of spilled oil, fishtailed wildly, and slid into the bales. March roared by into fifth place.

He began to push harder, moving up on Quavale, lapping slower machines, using the car as a fencer uses a foil, darting and slashing around the 2.1 mile circuit.

Quavale fell back with every curve. Out of three March drew abreast and passed the big Kurtis in a short, savage burst of speed, using every inch of the narrow blacktop to get by. He was fourth.

By God, you've taken one of the really hot boys. Let's keep moving. He could see Jerry Wyndham in the blue Maserati breaking early for turn six, and Randy's pit board told him the story. Wyndham was running out of brakes! Okay, then, let's get him!

Brake, downshift, accelerate, upshift, accelerate, brake. Over and over until his wrists ached, until his mouth was cotton-dry and his eyes burned through the dusty goggles. Closing. Closing.

And behind March, another threat. Sifting masterfully through the pack, Lou Coppard had driven his black Cad

Special to within a quarter-lap of March. Since the tire change, Coppard had passed all of the slower cars and was trying for another bid.

I can hold Lou, March told himself; he hasn't enough time to catch me unless something goes on the Merc. So, let's get that Maserati!

Wyndham was forced to slide through the curves, skimming the haybales with his rear wheels, fighting for control. March picked up another foot out of the third turn.

The two cars swept into the back straight, a pair of twin projectiles shot from giant cannon. March's foot was hard to the floor, a part of the machine itself, draining every ounce of power from the laboring engine. Through the separate leather flesh of the driving gloves he felt the wheel's rock-firmness in his hands.

I can take him at the end of the straight, March decided. He'll have to back off early to save what little brake he has left, and I'll pass him into the turn.

As the 5-4-3-2-1 cut-off markers leaped at them, Wyndham's brake lights went on and March blistered past, stabbed the brake pedal, snapped a quick downshift and drifted the turn, all four tires screaming. Wyndham fell in behind him.

With fifteen minutes remaining in the race, Robert March was third.

Randy's pit board told him he was almost three-quarters of a lap behind the second-place Monza of Jeffry Moore, and was about to be lapped by the leading D-Jag.

At least he'd been able to make Glenn and Randy proud

of him, and of the Special. Now all he had to do was hold.

March saw the D coming up fast in the rear-view mirror. Fischer would lap him into turn three, so March cut wide for the turn, braked early, and waved him in.

Engine howling, Fischer scalded by. March saw the Jag's brake lights wink on as Fischer began his slide. Suddenly, at the apex of the turn, the black car seemed to explode. Orange fame gouted from the engine compartment, and Fischer, blinded by smoke, lost control, mashing into the stacked bales, bursting through in fiery petals of burning hay.

March slowed, saw Fischer leap from the twisted machine, saw the flagmen rush forward with extinguishers – and then he was around the next turn and moving away. Robert March was second.

Look at your hands, March told himself, look at them! You're trembling like a novice in his first race. He felt the sweat, sour on his lips and under his goggles, felt it flushing over his body like a coating of warm oil. Fischer's okay. He's all right, so come out of it and drive. *Drive*!

He glanced in the rear-view mirror. Coppard! The flying Special was only a car-length behind him. Lou had taken neat advantage of Fischer's spin to move up fast.

As they flashed by the pits Randy held the board high and a single, hastily chalked word stood out in bold relief against the black: GO!

March, furious at his own weakness, began to drive deeper into the turns, braking at the last possible instant, drifting to the edge of the bales. Coppard, unable to maintain the pace, dropped back. Ten minutes remaining; ten minutes to hold his position.

Then March saw the red Ferrari of Jeffry Moore off the track and deserted! The car had thrown a front wheel and Moore had retired. With a cold shock of surprise Robert March realized he was now in first place!

So, he thought, you've driven the Special, the car they all laughed at, the car that never finished, into the lead – and they're all behind you, Waring and Quavale and Coppard, all of them. An hour ago all you wanted to do was finish and look at you now. Winning.

Winning!

As he roared over the sun-splashed macadam, under the dark wash of trees, past the flickering faces of the cheering crowd, Robert March felt suddenly cold; a chill sense of loss began to build within him.

If he won this race, March knew, things would never be the same. If he won today, his victory could never be erased in the minds of the crowd. He would no longer be "ole Doc," the poor, unlucky guy to cheer for, he would be the man to beat. A winner had to keep on winning. If I take this race they'll say, "He did it once, why can't he do it again?" How many times would Wyndham's brakes fail, or Fischer's Jag catch fire, or Moore's Ferrari throw a wheel – all in the same race? Sure, today had been a freak affair from the beginning, but that wouldn't matter to the crowd. And it wouldn't matter to Randy or Glenn. They'd want to see me do it again, and when I lost I'd just be a fool in a slow car. I just can't let myself win today.

Starter Al Tucker gave him the blue flag as he passed the main grandstand. One more lap to go.

Robert March made up his mind. If you've got no business at the head of the table, move aside for the man who has.

It would be simple, really. All he needed to do was keep his foot on the gas for a second too long. Every curve has a ragged edge. If you push your car beyond the ragged edge, beyond the point of minimum tire adhesion, you lose control. Beyond the ragged edge you spin out, and there is nothing you can do about it.

Let Coppard have the race. If his luck held, March could re-enter and finish behind the leaders.

Coming down the back straight at full-throttle, Robert March watched the cut-off markers growing in the distance. 110 miles per hour. Tiny dots, growing larger with speed. 112. Becoming sharp and legible. 115. Easily readable now. His speedometer needle bumped 120 miles per hour.

When he was certain that he could never make the turn, when he was sure he had held the pedal down long enough, Robert March tramped the brake, downshifted, snapping the stubby gear-lever into place, and began his drift.

He caught a single, quick glimpse of Lou Coppard entering the far end of the straight. Okay, Lou, take her. She's yours.

He felt the car breaking away into the long slide which would carry it into the bales. Now he was no longer master, no longer in control; he was simply a weight the machine carried with it toward the packed bales, a soft, helpless weight which could be crushed instantly to death or burned to sudden ash.

And then, in that long, dream-like slide, March realized why he was allowing this to happen. Because he was *afraid*.

He was afraid of the truth about racing and what it actually meant in his life. He'd kept it carefully hidden from Linda and the boys, even from himself, but now he faced it.

You race for only one reason, March told himself. Not just to prove you can finish with a car you built yourself, not to have the crowds cheer because they feel sorry for you – you race to win. You really didn't know, until today, if you had the guts to get out and drive the way a winner must drive. Now you know. You proved you can match the best of them, so it's time to stop fooling yourself. You're in racing because you've *got* to be in it, because it's a thing you love – and if you throw away your big chance now you'll keep on being afraid to do what you really want to do. You were worried about Linda, about what she would say, but remember her words before the race: *"Whatever you really want is what I want too."* You stuck with the Special because you knew it wouldn't win, because you could put the truth aside in such a car. How could you win if you never finished? Jeffry Moore had been right when he told you to get the Ferrari.

So, all right. Why throw this race when you have it in the palm of your hand? Win today and then buy that Ferrari Boucher has for sale. Drive this damn car out of the turn and take the checkered flag because that's what you've wanted all along. Let's GO!

In that timeless, suspended instant between the beginning and the end of the slide, all these thoughts flickered through his mind like quick images on a screen.

Then the Special's rear deck struck the first bale. March felt the car tipping, poised for a roll, and he instinctively lowered his head. But the Special maintained balance. It crashed back on its wheels, spun around twice and slid to a smoking halt, facing the straight, the engine stalled and silent.

Down the straight at full-bore came Lou Coppard, leaning over the wheel, a crooked victory grin on his grease-blackened face.

The flagmen were frantically waving March back on the circuit; another second and it would be too late.

If only she fires, breathed March, punching the starter button, if only the bales didn't finish her! With a dry cough, the Mercury came to life and Robert March bulleted onto the track just as Coppard began his drift.

The scream of the crowd was lost in the savage thunder of racing engines as the two cars roared out of the turn wheel to wheel.

Lou Coppard had the edge. With a stabbing burst of acceleration, he passed March out of the bend into the front straight.

Far ahead, the late afternoon sun glinting on the gaudy silk of his shirt, Al Tucker crouched with the checkered flag ready at his side, squinting down the long strip of blacktop at the two leaders.

Coppard, his mouth now hard and unsmiling, his foot mashing the pedal, led March by half a car-length at the pits, but it was not enough. In the final one hundred feet, with the crowd wild and shouting his name, Robert March edged past the streaking black Cad Special to take the checkered flag.

The Pebble Beach Del Monte Cup was his.

He saw them coming, Linda and the boys, running across the track to meet him as he rolled the Special slowly into the winner's circle.

He wasn't sure exactly what he would say to Linda. How do you tell a woman that you've suddenly discovered another force in your life as strong as she is – that you need both, deeply, genuinely, each in a different way?

Robert March watched his wife push through the crowd, waving, smiling, tears in her eyes, and he thought: perhaps I won't have to tell Linda anything.

Perhaps she already knows.

THIS STORY ALSO DEALS, IN PART, WITH automobile racing, but from an entirely different era.

My father, Michael Cahill Nolan, was a genuine automotive pioneer. He drove the first motor car over the wagon-rutted Santa Fe Trail from Kansas City (the Trail's originating point) into New Mexico, managed the Elm Ridge racing track in Missouri, and competed against the legendary Barney Oldfield. In fact, all of what the old man talks about in "Just Like Wild Bob" actually happened. It is my father's true history; only the fictional situation is invented. (Dad never compared me to Wild Bob Burman!)

When U.K. editor Peter Haining read "Just Like Wild Bob," in consideration for his noir anthology, *Mysterious Motoring Stories*, his first impulse was to reject the story since it did not fit his horror/fantasy theme. But, as he told me, he couldn't get it out of his mind, finding it "quite irresistible."

He felt compelled to add it to the contents – and "Just Like Wild Bob" became the only mainstream tale in the book.

My father was in the final stage of his life when I wrote my biography of *Barney Oldfield*, and dedicated the book to him.

I'm very happy to say that he lived long enough to see it published.

JUST LIKE WILD BOB

IT WAS HOT, desperately hot in the Ford, and McAllister felt the heat under his clothes, felt the perspiration gathering beneath his armpits and along his trousered thighs. Damn the California sun, he thought, and damn having to drive through it in an old heap of a '51 Ford with 90,000 wearing miles on the odometer.

He looked over at his father, who sat bolt upright in the heat, as straight as a soldier. And Paul McAllister thought: nothing bothers him, he just sits there in this blast-furnace air and nothing bothers him at all. My God, I hope things like heat and cold and long rides bother me when I'm eighty; I hope to God they do. He isn't even human. He's some kind of insensitive machine that keeps on operating no matter what happens to it. People look at him and say: isn't he wonderful, isn't it *grand* to be that way? And I feel like yelling at them, McAllister thought. I feel like yelling: if you think he's so damn wonderful and grand why don't you take him to live with you? Why don't *you* put up with his senility and his deafness and his dirt? You'd soon find out how grand he is.

Highway 99 ribboned ahead of them, flat and gray-white, rippling slightly in the heat-haze. Paul held the Ford at sixty-five. Not fast on a week day like this with no cops out, but plenty fast for the old Ford. It rolled and heaved drunkenly around curves and on a straight like this it took both hands to keep it steady at anything over fifty.

The thing is, I should have gone to San Berdoo without him, McAllister told himself; I should have said: hell no you can't go with me! This is business and I have to see this guy about something you wouldn't understand.... But his father had begged to be taken along, whined like a puppy, and McAllister had given in. Hours up and hours back in the August heat with the sun strong enough to suck the water from a camel's hump – but the old man had not complained once. He knew better. If he said a word McAllister would cut him to pieces with his tongue. He'd done it often enough before.

I'm thirty-one and he's eighty and he's got no business messing up my life, McAllister's inner monologue contin-ued. I ought to be married, have a wife and family of my own – and maybe I would if it weren't for him. Oh, well, I guess I wouldn't, but hell, who knows, really, whether I would or not? He's always there, around the house all day like some kind of vulture, crouched over the TV, maybe an inch from the screen because of his eyes, always giving me terrible suggestions about how to sell real estate, about what to say to people.

If Mother were alive things might be different. They *would* be, no doubt of it. She'd let him talk to her while she ironed or cooked and the words would go on past her because she never really listened to him, never really heard the same tired, dreadful stories over and over. The words would disappear in her mind like invisible ink on white paper.

But with her gone, he's just got me. Only me. And I can't ignore him the way Mother could. When I'm home he's talking all the time and I keep wanting to tell him to shut up, to shut his damn old mouth up, that I've heard all he's got to say a million times and just can't stand the words any longer. And sometimes, McAllister told himself with a bitter satisfaction, sometimes I *do* just that. I yell like fury at him and he shuts up for maybe an afternoon – or even an entire day – and pouts like a slapped kid.

The old man coughed violently next to McAllister. He pulled a gray handkerchief from his pants pocket and began to dab at his watering eyes with it.

"My God, *look* at that thing!" snapped McAllister. "I told you to make sure you had a clean one before you left."

"Sorry," the old man said, and smiled toothlessly. "Sorry, son, but I forgot to get another one from the drawer. I did."

"All right," Paul sighed. "But just put it away. You'll fill the car with germs."

McAllister's father nodded in the heat, his long yellow-white hair pasted thinly to his lined forehead. He looked over at his son and attempted another smile, but to Paul it was a grimace, a toothless grimace – and, perversely, Paul did not smile back.

"You didn't *have* to go along, you know," he told his father, eyes coldly fastened on the road ahead. "I warned you about the heat."

The old man seemed puzzled. "I didn't say nothing about the heat did I?" he asked. "I didn't say nothing."

McAllister sighed again and kept his eyes on the wide, flat highway running up into the hills. Sweat had gathered like a cluster of tiny seed-pearls on his upper lip and he ran the edge of his left sleeve over the skin, immediately angry with himself for not using his clean handkerchief and showing his father what it meant to carry fresh, laundered things.

Hell, he'd live like a pig if I ever left him, McAllister assured himself. He never washes really well, just kind of *pats* some water over him when he's in the tub. His bath towel shows it. Why is it that old people are so dirty? Not all of them, though. My grandfather on my mother's side was as neat as a pin right up to the day he died. And he was eighty-three. Yet most old people would live like pigs if they could.

A half-mile ahead of them, near the right side of the highway, McAllister made out a small figure, waving. As they drew nearer he braked to forty-five and squinted for a clearer look. A boy of maybe eighteen in blue denims with sandy, crew cut hair was waving and shouting something. Just a few feet behind the boy, completely off the highway on the grass verge, McAllister saw a light-green panel truck.

Gas, that's it, thought Paul; the kid's out of gas.

"There's a guy stuck up ahead," McAllister told his father. "I'm going to stop and give him a lift."

"Fine with me," the old man replied. "That's all right."

Paul had never believed in picking up hitchhikers. Never can tell about them. Maybe only one in a thousand's a sour apple, but he might be the one you pick up. Might be he's got a gun and he needs your car for some kind of getaway. But not this kid, McAllister was certain, not this kid here in the middle of the open highway in broad daylight with his own panel truck. Not a chance in a million. I'd be a heel if I passed him by.

McAllister brought the Ford to a halt by the truck and motioned to the boy in the denims. "Need a ride?" he asked.

"Sure do, mister," answered the boy, trotting over to the car. "Ran plain out of gas about a mile back and just coasted this far hoping I'd make a station. But don't seem like there's one around for miles."

"That's right," said Paul. "Nearest station is a good bit up the highway. Hop in, I'll take you. It's on the way."

"Thanks a lot," the boy said and was about to open the front door when Paul said: "Get in back. More room there."

"Okay." The boy slid into the rear of the Ford, slamming the door. McAllister accelerated away, leaving the green panel truck parked and silent behind them in the heat.

"My name is Springer," the boy said from the back seat. "Anson Springer."

"Mine's Paul McAllister," said Paul mechanically, watching the road. "This is my father."

"Hi," said the boy.

"Glad to make your acquaintance," smiled the old man, twisting in the seat and extending one withered yellow hand. The boy shook it briskly. "Same here."

"You work around these parts?" the old man asked – and Paul thought: hell, he's got someone to listen to him now and he's going to start talking up a storm. Maybe picking up this kid was a lousy idea after all. Dad knows when I'm sore and he stays quiet, but give him an extra pair of ears to bend and off he goes.

"I'm a mechanic in L.A.," replied the boy. "I help my brother in his garage."

"Then…you know cars, eh boy?" The old man twisted even farther around in the seat.

"Yeah, a little I guess." He hesitated. "I can take an engine apart if that's what you mean."

"Ever hear about a car called the Stevens-Duryea?" The old man's voice held a trace of urgency, of tenseness, and McAllister drew in a sharp breath and swore silently. God, he's going to start the business about the early days; he's going to go into the whole long, involved, exhausting bit.

"I doubt if he's ever heard of the car, Dad," said Paul, forcing a degree of pleasantness into his voice. He flicked his glance to the rearview mirror, hoping the boy would back up his statement. If so, the talk could be slanted, pushed away from the familiar subject at hand.

"As a matter of plain fact," the boy grinned, "I sure have. I mean, I've seen pictures of it. My brother's an old-car bug. Knows all about Barney Oldfield and like that."

From the corner of his eye McAllister could see his father straighten in triumph and nod quickly like a bird, the wrinkles on his veined neck folding deeply one upon another. It was too late now. When the boy mentioned Barney Oldfield McAllister realized it was too late.

"I knew him," piped the old man, still nodding. "Yes sir, I knew Barney. I raced against him when he drove a White Steamer in Missouri. Big White Steamer down in Missouri. Cross-country it was, maybe 200 miles, through mud so deep you could swim in it. I was in a Chalmers-Bluebird then and I let Barney break ground for me. I mean following his big Steamer, staying right in his tracks while all the other cars bogged down. Near the end of the race old Barney he ran out of water and had to stop and leave his car on the road while he went into a farmhouse and asked for some. For the Steamer, you know. Had to have water for the Steamer."

Paul made one more desperate attempt. "Maybe he doesn't want to hear all about that stuff, Dad," McAllister said, his voice now edged and crisp. "It's a pretty damn hot day and maybe–"

"Oh no, I'm glad to listen," the boy cut in. "Golly!… Al – that's my brother, Al – he'll be mighty surprised when I tell him I met somebody that actually raced Barney Oldfield. Did you finally beat him, Mr. McAllister?"

Paul sighed and kept his eyes fixed on the road. It was no use, none at all, and now all he could hope for was a gas station. He pressed his foot down on the pedal and the speedometer needled up to sixty-eight, then seventy. The

Ford began to shudder and Paul eased off. No use wrecking the car just to keep from hearing it all again, he thought. Won't be much longer. We'll get there soon. I know there's a new station opened up about five miles or so down the highway.

"Well, I never *did* beat ole Barney," his father was saying. "I passed him when he went for water that time, but my car threw a rod and I never finished that race at all. Ole Barney, he won fair an' square."

I doubt if Oldfield ever drove a White Steamer, McAllister thought bitterly. Sure, you probably raced a couple of times, but I bet you never came any closer to Oldfield than a sparrow comes to a hawk.

"I knew Bobby Burman, too," the old man went on, warming to his subject. His eyes began to water under the wrinkled lids and he blinked rapidly. "We called him Wild Bob because he was a regular hellion behind the wheel. This was 1909 you know, and he used to come out to Missouri and race at the Elm Ridge track." The old man took out his gray handkerchief and scrubbed at his watering eyes.

Filthy, thought McAllister; that's just plain filthy. You can't tell an old man anything. Tell him to keep that thing out of sight and he'll be blowing his nose with it in front of the Queen of England five minutes later! Like a three-year-old. You can't tell them anything they remember.

"Wild Bob was in a Stoddard-Dayton out at Elm Ridge one Sunday," the old man continued, "and it was beginning to rain cats and dogs. Well, Bobby was cuttin' up the track, you know, with that big car of his, and so I went out to flag him down. I was chairman of the racing committee then and we didn't want the track all cut up in the rain. We'd have a real bad time packing it all down again if he cut it up and so I tried to flag him and get him off there."

Who cares, thought McAllister, Dear Lord who the hell cares what happened forty-nine lousy years ago on some lousy dirt track in Missouri? He's failed at everything he ever tried in his life, lost all my mother's money, made her sell our house to invest in one of his crazy schemes and lived just as he wanted to live, not caring for what other people wanted, what my mother wanted, or me, or anyone. He's a failure and I hope to God I'm never like him. But to hear him talk you'd think he was a big, raging success at everything. From auto racing to raising chickens...I'll bet he never won a race in his life, Paul thought, never in his life.

"So he hits me," the old man was saying, his voice droning on in the heat, behind McAllister's thoughts. "He skidded, comes sideways across the wet track and hits me." The old man threw up a leathery hand. "Knocked me ten feet in the air and broke every bone in my body. Even today I got a plate in my left leg that aches when it rains." He tapped the spot. "Silver plate just like on a dinner table. Right here in my leg."

"Golly...that's something," said the boy from the rear seat. McAllister found it impossible to tell whether he was simply bored and being polite or whether he really wanted to hear more of this.

"They put me in the morgue. Left me for dead!" The old man nodded again, chuckling with a sound like wind in high grass. A rustling, repulsive kind of chuckle, thought McAllister.

"But I woke up and threw off that sheet and crawled across that cold floor to the feller in charge and scared him half to death. They took me to the hospital and I was out and walking in two weeks!"

Yes, and tell him about your fistula and your ulcers and the cancer you got over like it was a cold in the head, McAllister silently prodded. Tell him how you're stronger even than God in his heaven! Roosevelt dies and Stalin and Ronald Colman but you go right on. Not human, that's all; you're just not human.

"I drove the Pathfinder car for the Star Cup Tour back in 1910," the old man said. "That was in the Stevens-Duryea I mentioned. We called 'er the Big Six and she was sixty horsepower. Steering her was like grabbing a wagon wheel and it took a mile to get her rolling good. But then she'd do eighty. Roads were gumbo in those days. We couldn't get her movin' very fast on those roads. I had the agency for Stevens-Duryea in Kansas City then and I was selected over forty other dealers to blaze the way for the Star Cup runners. I mean, I drove the whole two thousand miles and we laid out the route for the auto tour that came later that year. We were the first car over the Glorietta mountains in New Mexico, first car to ever travel the Old Santa Fe trail." Paul's father was caught up afresh in the emotion of the Golden Era, and McAllister wondered where in hell that new gas station was, how many more miles they had to go before the kid could be dumped and the conversation terminated.

"Oh, we had ourselves a *time*," the old man chuckled. He needed a shave and the sun picked up the spiny edge of beard along his lower jaw. "Dust, gumbo, rocks so big it took the four of us to move 'em, rain and cold and roads like goat trails. Had ten rainstorms the first two and a half days out of Kansas City. But we made it, the whole way and back, and when we rolled into Kansas they tied wheat to the sides of the Big Six and we came on into Missouri, into Kansas City, and the crowds were out in the streets shouting at us and cheering and yelling our names...." The old man's voice dimmed away into memory.

"Didn't you have any breakdowns?" asked the boy.

"None major. We never missed an explosion in all the two thousand miles. I mean, the engine didn't. Ran like a clock. I tell you if they ran like they used to they wouldn't need mechanics like you these days. Young buck like you could get out and hustle for work 'cuz there just wouldn't be none if the cars were all like my Big Six. Oh, we broke a wheel in the Gloriettas, but we got her changed quick enough. Had to use a mule team to haul us outa one big mudhole in Colorado but she never missed an explosion. No sir, she never missed."

Ahead of them, near a broad intersection, McAllister spotted the gas station. Thank God, he thought, for the sign of the Flying Red Horse! Never looked so good to me before. And just in time, too, or else he would have gone into the business of his entering the Star Cup tour and leading most of the way and then breaking down near the end and the whole long bit. I couldn't take that, thought

McAllister, as he approached the intersection, I just couldn't take that. A cream-colored Oldsmobile was moving rapidly out of the station and Paul had to twist the wheel and hardbrake to avoid him.

"Well, here we are," he said to the boy. "You can get a can of gas and hitch a ride back to your truck with no trouble."

"Thanks, thanks a lot, mister," said the boy, jumping out and slamming the car door behind him. "And…" He hesitated, looking into the seamed face of the old man. "I sure do want to thank you for telling me about Barney Oldfield and all. I'll tell Al when I get back to L.A. and he'll have a fit he wasn't along. He'll just have himself a plain fit he didn't meet you."

They shook hands, Paul's father and the teenaged boy in blue denims – and just before the boy was about to turn away the old man raised an ivoried hand and gripped Paul's shoulder. "You see the way my boy handles this Ford? You see him whip it in here and miss that other feller? Handles this Ford like it was a kiddy car. Well, now, he drives, don't he? I watch him and I think of the way Wild Bob used to drive and I'm proud. Cuz he's just like him. My son here drives just like Wild Bob."

"I'll see ya," the boy said, and he waved as Paul rolled the car back onto the long flat highway.

"Nice youngster," the old man said, and he folded his bony arms across his chest. He coughed once and lapsed into silence.

In the mid-day heat, driving the tired Ford toward Los Angeles, Paul McAllister tried not to think about his father, or 1910, or a car named the Stevens-Duryea, or a man they called Wild Bob. And, most particularly, he tried not to think of the compliment his father had paid him, of the words and the pride behind the words. The old man had no business saying a thing like that and making him feel the way he suddenly felt. It threw everything out of perspective; it didn't fit the pattern.

I didn't ask him for it, McAllister thought angrily, I didn't *want* him to say it.

But the words of pride had been spoken and although McAllister gripped the wheel tighter and pressed harder on the gas pedal the rush of highway and the heat and his own inner voice telling him to forget, to ignore the words, failed. They failed to dull the sudden ache within his chest, the pain that stabbed at him from a place he could never hope to reach.

Beside him, sitting as straight as a soldier, his father produced the gray handkerchief and scrubbed at his watering eyes.

WHEN "ENCOUNTER WITH A KING" was initially printed in *Knight*, the editor boldly announced it to readers as "one of the most realistic fight stories ever published." Ray Bradbury wrote to me the day after it appeared, praising the story as "amazing…something I could never have written." And in testimony to its authenticity, it was chosen for inclusion (alongside classics by Ernest Hemingway, Jack London, Budd Schulberg, Ring Lardner, Arthur Conan Doyle, and other giants) for *In the Ring: A Treasury of Boxing Stories*.

All of which is ironic because, when I wrote "Encounter With a King," I had absolutely no first-hand knowledge of boxing. I had never attended a prize fight, had never laced on a pair of boxing gloves. The "realism" came strictly from research – Serling's *Requiem for a Heavyweight*, Kirk Douglas in *Champion*, Schulberg's *The Harder They Fall*.

The story emerged from character and emotion.

I wanted to dramatize the conflict between youth and age, and it seemed to me that an ideal way to do this was to center my story around the killer instinct inherent in the blood sport of boxing. How would a tough young contender deal with a fading champion? As one career begins, another ends. In writing "Encounter With a King," I saw a chance to examine this endless cycle of life in a fresh light.

Here is my first – and no doubt my last – boxing tale.

I've still never been to a prize fight.

ENCOUNTER WITH A KING

ASIDE FROM THE RAW CIRCUS FLASH of the "Dancer WEBB vs. King SOLAMAN" fight poster newly tacked to the pitted screen door, the Hot Shot Eatery was like a thousand other timeworn roadside cafes in Kansas. Beneath a twist of dirt-streaked neon a rusting red metal DRINK COCA COLA sign clung stubbornly to the flaking wind-eroded clapboard front, and an opaque sheen of grease clouded the two plate glass windows.

Inside, at the end of the long wooden lunch counter, Anthony T. Webb sat on a peeling oilcloth covered stool, talking to the waitress. He had been called "Dancer" since his sophomore year in high school because whenever he fought – and fighting was his business – he moved fast, on the balls of his feet, dancing in on his target, striking, and dancing away. Fast. Fast and light.

"I recognized you right off from the poster," the waitress

said, dabbing idly at the counter top with a frayed cloth. "Read all about you in today's paper…" (Cute girl, Dancer noted, real cute, with a neat little figure under her plain white uniform. Blue eyes, brown soft hair. Nice.) "The sports page told all about how you're supposed to beat this Solaman guy tonight. Tells all about you."

As Dancer listened, he thought: poor kid's probably lonely as hell out here in a Kansas tank town like Railton, with nothing to do but serve coffee and burgers to local characters. Dancer knew he looked real good to her with his sharp Chicago suit and his handsome unmarked face framed by blond curly hair. I must look like something right out of the movies to this kid, he thought. So okay. So let's see if we can wrap this one up, this little no-ring-on-her-finger lonesome-type doll.

"Ever watch the fights?" asked Dancer, lazily raising his head like a cat to smile at her.

She said she didn't. "I'm a baseball nut. I dunno anything about boxing."

"Not much to know," said Dancer. "Like, take tonight. I put on a pair of gloves, and I hit a guy. He ends up on his back and I get paid for putting him there."

The girl's eyes widened. "Then – this is one of those 'fixed' fights?"

Dancer chuckled. "No, it's on the square. But putting away an old plowhorse like Solaman is no problem."

"Why do you fight a man if you know you can beat him?"

"Because that's how it's done. When you win you move

up. And right now I'm moving up."

Sometimes a question like this bothered him. Sometimes, in the early morning hours when sleep was away on the other side of the horizon, Dancer wondered about his real direction in life; his future didn't seem as clear as it should be. Fighting was a dirty game, and the dirt didn't always wash away. But he should be used to it by now. You live with dirt to get where you have to go.

The girl said: "More coffee?"

Dancer leaned forward toward her over the counter. "Look," he said, "I got an extra ticket for tonight." He handed her a small white envelope. "Be my guest, eh?"

The girl hesitated a moment, looking at the envelope. Then she smiled back at him. "Thanks," she said.

Dancer knew he excited her, but she wasn't completely sold yet. After she saw him in action tonight, with his lithe, hard-muscled boxer's body moving smooth as oil up there under the ring lights, when she saw him put away old Solaman sweet as a baby in a crib and heard the crowd cheer his name, *then* she'd be sold. And after the fight he'd have time enough for her before the train to K.C. Just enough time for this lonely little doll.

Dancer checked his watch. Spec and Patchey would be here soon, and he'd agreed to meet them in front of the cafe. "After the fight we'll go somewhere and relax a little," he told the girl while she rang up the sale. "Okay?"

"Sure – okay," she said. "See you."

Dancer walked to the door, knowing she was watching every step he took. Smiling, he opened the screen and stepped into the blaze of Kansas sunlight.

Outside the Hot Shot, Dancer studied the poster announcing his bout with Solaman: Anthony Theodore "Dancer" Webb, 22, unmarried, weight 156. Style: fast and weaving. Record to date: 15 bouts, 13 wins. Potential: the middleweight crown.

Actually, thought Dancer, the record should stand at fourteen wins out of fifteen. The first loss, back in the beginning, was ordinary enough, and could happen to any young fighter on the way up: he'd lacked the savvy and was overmatched. So – a K.O., lights out. But the other one should never have happened, and an odd feeling of guilt lay behind it. A bean-legged kid named Zuckerman had nailed him, three months ago in Cincy because…damn it, because the kid looked like his brother Tom, who'd been killed over-seas, and hitting the kid was like hitting his own flesh. That weakness in himself, that sudden inability to punch, had cost him the fight. But that was a freak thing, meeting a guy who looked like Tommy, and it would never happen again. So why couldn't he forget it? Why the hell keep thinking about it?

The sound of tires on gravel startled Dancer. A battered red and yellow taxi rolled to a stop near the cafe. A voice from the car window said: "Been waiting long, kid?"

Webb turned toward his manager, Spec Leonard, who was now holding the rear door open. Dancer could see Patchey Johnson inside, smiling at him. "We couldn't find a cab in this hick burg," said Patchey.

"No problem," Dancer told them. "Let's go."

And he did not look back at the poster as he climbed into the taxi.

"We got things all set for tonight," Leonard said when Dancer had settled into the seat. "You work out with Patchey in the downtown gym for awhile to loosen up, then you catch a couple hours sleep before the match."

Spec Leonard, with his close-cropped bullet head was one of those ageless people in the sport who could be forty or fifty – or maybe thirty-five when the sun was down. He never told you and you never asked. Spec had handled some of the best. Red Garvey had been one of his boys, and Omaha Charlie Ross and Dutch Nielson and Kid Latimar. He'd taken them on when they were awkward punks with six arms and made them great. Patchey Johnson had introduced Dancer to Leonard. "Here's the next champ," he'd said. "You manage him, I train him, and the kid'll go all the way."

Fat and rosy-cheeked, Johnson was a calculating man under his loud façade of humor and fast talk. Single-minded and unrelenting in his profession, he trained fighters to do one thing only: to win – and that meant no cigarettes or liquor or late hours in town with their women; that meant roadwork and the rope and the bags; that meant a steady unbroken string of days at camp with no easing off, no break in the toughening rhythm. You worked like hell for Patchey Johnson because you knew he would settle for nothing less.

"Don't be so sure of this guy," Spec Leonard told them, pulling the red tab and twisting the cellophane from a pack of Luckies. "He may be over the hill but he's got plenty of savvy and he can still put out the lights with that big left of his if he gets the chance."

"Yeah, and like when has that been lately?" asked Patchey.

"Like two months ago in Ohio when he flattened Sid Blanchard."

Patchey snorted. "Blanchard's a second-rater. He's lucky he can stand up without a crutch. Dancer can take this Solaman tonight with one glove. Right, kid?"

Dancer nodded – but he was remembering when, not so long ago, the man he would fight this evening, this man called "King" Solaman, had been at the top. A king indeed, with the middleweight crown to prove it. A compact dark mass of fighting flesh that took all the punishment there was to be taken and then found an opening and moved in with that single killing powerhouse left. But the not-so-long-ago had been six years, and now Solaman was almost thirty-nine, tired and old and with too much punishment from too many blows behind him.

"You take Solaman, then we go for Geha in K.C.," said Patchey. "Then we're movin', we're really *movin'*. Detroit, L.A. Maybe the Garden by the end of the year. Who knows, eh? Maybe the Garden."

"You talk like he was already champ," said Spec, stubbing out his cigarette on the window of the cab. "Boy's gotta walk before he can run."

"He don't need to run," grinned Patchey. "He *dances* to the top, this kid!"

"Right now just let him worry about the King a little,"

finished Spec.

Patchey raised his head, giving them both his broad smile. "That's just how much he'll worry," he said, "a little."

As Dancer moved toward the heavy swinging bag in the corner of Lacey's Health Club he thought about how much he hated this flat, dry country, with its killing heat and lousy hotels. He was born in Chicago and to Chicago. The cutting wind on Michigan Avenue was a sweet wine to Dancer Webb – and the Loop, brash and loud and fast-moving, was his special playground. Chicago had guts and flare and a will of its own. It was like a woman, sometimes you had to *take* what you wanted, not ask for it, because she was giving nothing away. But Kansas was a pushover. Just like that little waitress back in the cafe. Soft and ready. Pushover. And tonight he'd push over another easy mark to get a little closer to where he had to go. The really rough stuff was ahead – in Kansas City and Detroit and the Garden. Not here. Not tonight.

Patchey had told him how to go after Solaman on the train coming out here. "You pound his belly and ribs," Patchey had said, grinning his fat grin and shaking that hound head of his. "You just go for the breadbasket, kid, cuz that's where he lives – he don't like it much down there. You work on him good down where it hurts, then you move upstairs and finish the job."

Now, slamming the heavy bag, Dancer pictured his antagonist, weakening under each hammer-blow, staggering under the barrage, with the crowd shouting for the knock-down, shouting his name…*Dancer! Dancer! Dancer!*

In his dressing room below stairs Dancer could hear the crowd, an immense rush of voices, rising and falling in pitch like waves on a shore. On this muggy Saturday night in Railton every seat was taken for the ten-round main, following the prelims. Right now, up there in the ring, two local boys were mixing it up. Two boys who had never been anywhere and would never get there.

With three hours of sleep behind him, shoes and silk trunks on, with the tape and the gloves ready, Dancer felt the old familiar surge of animal power singing in his blood. He knew he'd win tonight. Like Patchey said, this one was a lock.

Yet, like a faint pulsebeat below his skin, something was bothering him about Solaman. He couldn't pin down the feeling; maybe later. Maybe.

A fuzz-faced cub reporter from the local paper was shooting questions at Dancer as Patchey carefully wound tape around the fighter's outstretched hand.

"How about a final statement?" the boy asked, "ya know, something that'll look good in print."

"Sure," grinned Patchey. "Just say that tonight Dancer Webb is gonna send King Solaman back to the mines."

The reporter jotted down the words, then confided, "Solaman's through after this one. The King is abdicating."

Dancer raised his eyes to the young reporter. "Where'd you hear that?"

"From his old lady – Mrs. Alonzo Solaman herself. I

talked to her before I came down and she says this is the last one for him. She seemed damn glad he was quitting."

So this is the end of the line, thought Dancer. Up from the Harlem slums to the top – and now the finish, here in a lousy Kansas tank town with the hicks screaming for blood. Well, you play the game and you've got to quit sometime.

Spec opened the door and motioned the reporter out.

"We're up," he said, handing Dancer his silk robe, bright red to match his trunks. "So let's go."

This was the moment the crowd had been waiting for: when the raking twin spots swept across a sea of expectant faces and steadied on the tall swing doors at either end of the arena.

The doors opened, and the two combatants stepped into the glare, into the crowd's roar and the massed heat of shouting, shifting close-packed bodies.

They moved down the aisles to the ring, Dancer, Spec, and Patchey to the right, Solaman and his boys to the left – each fighter towel-hooded like a monk, each moving leisurely toward the roped canvas carved by the white flare of lights. They wore bright silk, with a single word stitched on the back of each robe: red silk, DANCER in gold; black silk, KING in silver.

As he neared his corner Dancer saw the girl from the cafe, sitting where he knew she would be sitting, looking fresh and summery in a light print dress accenting her full figure. He winked at her as he passed and she gave him back a warm smile in return. Tonight, thought Dancer as he ducked through the ropes, I've got an extra reason for looking good. To the victor…

After Solaman had shrugged aside his robe Dancer looked closely at his enemy. (That was the way Spec told him to think of a man in the ring: an enemy to be conquered before he conquered you.)

Solaman had his back to Dancer, executing a little shuffling step, muscles moving under his skin like sleek fish in bronze waters. Now he turned, and Dancer thought: he's still got it, whatever it takes to make a champion. He may be old and soft, but he's still got that look – like he doesn't belong to the human race, like he's something special.

I wonder how many of them out there tonight can still recognize it. A few of them maybe, but not many. They're here to see youth defeat age, to see white against black, to see some royal blood spilled.

To the far left, near Solaman's corner, *his* part of the crowd had gathered. Dark men and women, not more than a dozen in all, his friends and his wife, there to see him fight for the last time, there to hope for some sudden miracle against this fast, deadly destroyer from Chicago.

The announcer was in the center of the ring, a red-necked fat man in a bow tie sweating through a starched white shirt. He was telling the crowd what they already knew about both fighters: the towns they came from, their weight, the color of their trunks, their full names, the maximum number of rounds in the bout – all the required information delivered like a political speech in measured dramatic tones, as standardized as a newsboy's chant.

Dancer took his bow to wild applause, but Solaman's expression did not alter as he accepted the subdued spatter of handclaps from his side of the arena.

The two men met silently in the center of the white square, heads lowered in an attitude of prayer as they listened to the fat man's droning voice, telling them to abide by the rules. "…and now shake hands, gentlemen, and come out fighting."

As Dancer touched gloves, he looked deep into Solaman's impassive eyes, seeing no emotion there that he could catalogue. Louis, the Brown Bomber, had looked like this; even when he was losing you could never see it in his eyes.

The sudden pre-fight hush before the bell, a heart beat of hot silence in the packed arena. Then the warning buzzer.

"Stay away from that left of his," Spec Leonard said, speaking with his close-shaven bullet head close to Dancer's ear. "He can still punch if you give him an opening. So wind him, keep him running. And go for the body."

At the bell, Dancer came out of his corner like a Jack-in-the-box propelled by a spring. He'd show them some style, some class; he'd let them see his famous legwork while he ran circles around this slow-moving dusky man who faced him now under the lights.

Solaman did not crouch to protect his body; he fought erect, as he had in the old days when body blows were only so many insect stings, when his massive frame could still take the punishment and come back for more. But now, when he should be covering up, he wasn't. Stubborn pride kept him tall, and Dancer knew he could finish the job in two rounds if he really tried.

The face of King Solaman was shiny with healed scar tissue. The nose and ears had lost sharp definition; under the force of a hundred ring encounters they had slowly retreated into the clay-colored face – just as the eyes had retreated under battered ledges of bone. They were incredibly dark eyes, cave-black, flecked with silver when the lights caught them, and they were fixed to the weaving, dipping, shifting figure of Dancer Webb.

Webb allowed a hard right to slide off his shoulder, slashing in with a left to the body, a right and another left, hard, to the body, then danced away from the return punches with that easy half-smile on his handsome unmarked face.

Someone in the crowd yelled: "Kill the bastard, Webb, *kill* him!"

Dancing, weaving, hooking, chopping, back-pedaling in and out, around and around, with Solaman shuffling heavily after him, taking the punches where they hurt with no trace of pain evident in that great impassive face.

Solaman had been good all right, Dancer told himself, as he felt the power of the King's left against his own rib cage; he's only half a man now, but when he fought the invincible Belanski to a standstill in the Garden and sent him down in that final, tension-filled ninth round – when he'd put away the big boys one by one: Tiger Altman, the Baltimore Ace, Aiken and Ted Roeburt, all of them – that's when he should have retired; not now, not tonight with the hicks waiting for his blood, waiting to see him crushed to the canvas. No, thought Dancer, you should have quit when they were still cheering you! I just hope to God I have enough sense to do that, he thought, dancing in again and going for the body, striking and dancing away. Yeah, I hope I still got that much sense left in my head when I get to the other side of the hill.

Then the bell rang and the first round was over. Already, Dancer knew, the King was tiring. By the end of the second he'd be ripe.

"You were *terrific*, kid," Patchey told him, working on his neck and back while Spec Leonard tipped up the bottle and Dancer swallowed, grateful for the cool liquid against his dry throat.

"I felt a couple," said Dancer. "He's still got a left."

"Sure," grinned Patchey, "if there's anything in front of him to hit. Maybe a wooden Indian he could put away!"

"How you feel?" asked Spec.

"Great. Think I should try to take him out in the second?"

Leonard shook his head. "Let it go three," he said. "They came for a show, so let's give 'em one. Stay on your bicycle. Dance him around in there. Then you can axe him at the end of the third."

"And remember the belly," Patchey reminded him, pulling away the stool at the buzzer. "Give it to him solid down there."

At the bell, Dancer moved out lightly on the balls of his feet. He knew the girl from the cafe was watching him, probably a little breathless with excitement, watching him move, sharp and quick, godlike under the lights. I've never looked better, he told himself.

Solaman followed Dancer in a shuffling series of flat-soled steps, waiting for a chance to use his legendary left, the powerhouse left that had put down so many of the greats. But Dancer wouldn't slow for it; he came weaving in like a shadow, connected with a flurry of punches, then darted back out of range. His slashing gloves had opened up an old scar above Solaman's right eye, and the King's lips were puffed and swollen over the mouthpiece. Dancer was beginning to work on the face as well as the body.

The crowd loved it, shouting for the kill, anxious to see Alonzo Solaman go down. Even the quiet group to the left of the arena, the King's friends – even *they* wanted it to be over. Every blow reached them; watching the two men – bright with perspiration up there in the bluewhite smoke haze – they sat almost unmoving, silent, waiting.

The dry-leaf scuff of shoes on canvas, the heavy wet smacking sound of leather on flesh, the unceasing voices yelling for blood, now high, now low, and the minutes ticking past on the official time clock: this was the fall of a king.

I'm still fresh and he's already badly winded, thought Dancer, rolling smoothly away from a left hook that grazed his cheek. He's wishing to God the bell would ring and he could sit down and rest, get his breath back, but the bell won't ring for another long minute and I won't give him time to get his breath.

In, out, slashing, thumping, cutting at the head and belly and ribs…

106

Dancer moved in again, thistle-light and fast on his toes, giving the crowd something to remember when they talked about the quick young kid from Chicago. He loosed a stunning combination of blows and Solaman reeled back, arms out, falling into a clinch against the ropes. The sharp odor of perspiration reached Dancer; he felt a trickle of warm blood on his shoulder from Solaman's swollen lips, and as he attempted to shove back the heavy-breathing coppery body the referee parted them – just as the bell ended round two.

"He's gonna go down like Oregon timber!" enthused Patchey, swabbing Dancer's face and chest. "You practically got him sleepwalking out there."

"He's old and he's tired and his wind is gone," said Dancer. "I'm not proving anything to anybody. What the hell am I proving?"

"Next round, you take him," said Spec Leonard, his eyes narrow and hard on Dancer's. "You go in and stretch him this time. Hear me?"

"I hear you," said Dancer.

But when the third round began, and Dancer saw the stolid, advancing figure of Alonzo Solaman moving toward him, erect and unafraid over the stretched white canvas, he began to ask himself questions; he began to examine an area within himself which he'd tried to ignore, tried to believe wasn't there at all. Did he have any right to do what he was doing? When I send him down tonight I'm sending down his pride, everything he lived for, everything people remember him for. When he goes down tonight that's how they'll think of him, flat on the deck, glaze-eyed and helpless as a baby – a bloody, beaten hulk to gloat over.

"Eat him up and spit him out, Dancer!" a woman shrilled from below. "Murder him!"

That's just what I'd be doing, Webb told himself, as he back-pedaled away from a chopping right; that's just what I'd be doing: murdering a king. Is this bout worth a man like Solaman? Is one lousy win in one lousy tank town in Kansas worth destroying a man like this? He could hear Patchey yelling at him. "The belly, Kid – go for the belly!"

But he didn't. Dancer flicked out a harmless right and ducked inside the return left, moving out of range.

One solid punch from the King would end it, he said to himself. Just let Solaman get that powerhouse left across solid and that would do it. No one could doubt the result, they'd all seen it happen a hundred times: that sudden opening and then the smashing, crushing left, straight in to the jaw, putting out the lights. That was all Solaman had now, that waiting terrible left, but he was no longer able to catch his man and use it. Not unless that man made a mistake.

It wouldn't be easy. He'd lose the girl out there in the darkness; a girl like that doesn't touch a loser. But it would be a chance to do a right thing instead of a wrong one, a chance to give instead of take. All his life he'd taken, like his father had taken when he walked out on the family so many years ago. Dancer had always taken everything he could get from life, from the girls he'd loved, but never *loved*, from his mother, from his friends… Now he could do one decent thing: he could give King Solaman this fight, a great victory to be remembered instead of an ignoble defeat. Oh, they'd talk about this one; they'd talk about the night the King came back from the grave to stop Dancer Webb cold in the third. They'd all talk plenty about this one.

His fighter's instinct told him no, that he was a fool, a crazy damn fool to be thinking this way. He'd been taught to avoid blows, not walk into them. This meant going directly against his grain, against everything he'd been trained for up to this moment. Could he really force himself to do it? He was afraid of that left, of the power of that terrible left, but there was no other way to do what he felt he had to do. It would have to be a case of conscious action over unconscious instinct…

The round was half over. Spec and Patchey were nodding their heads with each blow Dancer drove home, mentally counting the seconds before Solaman would fall. Then, abruptly, a shocked cry stabbed up from the arena. Patchey put one hand to his mouth. "My God!" he said.

For suddenly King Solaman had struck. He'd found an opening; miraculously it was there – and the mighty left had crashed into Webb's jaw like a boulder into sand. Dancer's head snapped back, his eyes rolled up white, and he fell – straight forward on his face to the hard gray canvas.

Alonzo Solaman, breathing hard, his face glittering with diamond specks, stepped back as the countdown began. Somewhere in the darkness to the left a woman's voice said: "Bless you, King!"

And when the rest of the crowd saw that it was over, that a great fighter had rallied to win over the fast brash boy from Chicago, they began to cheer for this exhausted giant. He was a champion again – and they were cheering for a champion.

Patchey didn't wait for the official verdict. He ducked under the ropes and ran toward his boy. But Spec Leonard did not move. He watched Dancer Webb stagger to his feet under Patchey's supporting hands, and still he did not move.

In the dressing room, under the raw overhead glare, Dancer was lying on his back on the long rubdown table and Patchey was cutting away the tape on his hands and talking soft and easy to him, as a mother talks to her child.

"He just got lucky is all," intoned the little man. "He just threw a lucky punch, Hell, you *had* him, kid. They all saw that. You had him all the way and then he just got lucky. That's all, he just got real, real lucky."

Spec had been silent since they'd left the ring. Now he stood over the table, watching the trainer work.

"I – I'm sorry, Spec," said Dancer, squinting up, attempting to clear his head of the pain that remained behind his eyes. His face was still handsome, but it was no longer unmarked.

"Don't give me that crap," snapped Leonard. "I saw what I saw."

Dancer sighed. "Okay, so I threw it – but what the hell, it's only one lousy fight. I just couldn't go out and slaughter that tired old bastard tonight. I just couldn't."

"That's right," said Leonard slowly, "you couldn't. And that's something for you to live with." He leaned closer to

Webb. "Do you believe that Solaman would ever do what you did tonight if *you* were at the bottom of the hill? Lemme tell you he wouldn't, not in a million years. Because he's hard, because he's got the stuff it takes to be a champ, with no room left for anything else. You weakened. I saw it in your eyes after the second round. Hell, I saw it on your face in Cincy when you let that Zuckerman punk dump you. Kid, you got a flaw in you. I guess I needed to be sure about it. Well – so now I'm sure."

Leonard turned, opened the door and hesitated for a moment. "You and me, Dancer, we've just said good-bye."

Then he was gone, the door bumping shut behind him.

As Patchey's confused voice rang in his ears Dancer closed his eyes against the light – knowing that he could never close his eyes against what he had done, knowing there wouldn't be any K.C. or Detroit or L.A. for him now, that he would never stand there in the Garden as a champion with the crowd shouting his name.

A crack had opened, a fault in his career that had been there all along, and it could never be closed.

"Listen, kid, don't you worry," Patchey was telling him. "Spec'll be back. Hell, he never walked out on a fighter yet. You watch, he'll be back."

"Sure," said Dancer softly, his eyes still closed, feeling the pain again, "he'll be back."

IN DECEMBER OF 1952, newly arrived in Los Angeles, I obtained a job as credit assistant in the Spring Street offices of the Blake, Moffitt & Towne paper company. I lived in Culver City at the time, and detested the traffic-clogged morning commute to downtown Los Angeles. Detested my job. Detested my boss – a sullen brute named Leo T. Cooney. He would stride in, dour-faced, at the start of each day and we (the credit department employees) were expected to greet him with a hearty "Good morning, Mr. Cooney." To which he never responded, just glared at us. After a few weeks of this, I greeted Cooney with the same sullen silence, glaring back at him.

This enraged the man. I wouldn't kiss ass, and I was discharged. Great! Free at last! The month after Cooney fired me I made my first short story sale. I was on my way out of Office Hell and into professional writing.

Yet, years after I was free, the horrors of office work, the helpless feeling of being an indentured slave, continued to haunt my mind. Finally, determined to exorcise my office demons, I sat down one afternoon and wrote "Two Coffees."

I became Billy Spiker, and the pain was real.

TWO COFFEES

THE WESTWOOD COFFEE SHOP was not crowded when the two of them came in. It was four in the afternoon, and even the late-lunch boys were back in the office.

They took a table near the wall, and when the waitress glided over to them the middle-aged man, Lanham, ordered. "Two coffees, please."

The girl nodded, scribbled on a pad, and moved back to the counter.

Sidney Lanham took out a package of Chesterfields and offered them.

"No, thanks," said the young man. His name was Billy Spiker.

Lanham removed a cigarette and sighed, turning the white cylinder slowly in his fingers. "You know, Billy," he said after an interval of silence, "I was talking to Mr. Allen about you."

"I figured you might have," said Billy Spiker, letting his eyes slide half-closed.

"Mr. Allen likes you. Hell, we all like you."

"Fine," said Billy.

"No knives in the back from Mr. Allen. If he doesn't like a man, he tells him to his face. Straight out."

"I guess Allen's all right," said Billy.

"Mr. Allen started with Moffitt and Dodson fifteen years ago in the stock room, then got into selling and took over the whole department in five years. Best salesman Moffitt and Dodson ever had. Sold way over his quota every season. Top M and D man five years in a row."

"I know all about him," Billy said. "They tell the new boys all about him."

Sid nodded his head. "Hell of a talent. An inspiration to every man at M and D."

Billy said nothing. He stared down at his folded hands.

"And he's got his eye on all of us. He knows our problems. He *worries* about us."

"And now he's worried about me," said Billy. "Is that it?"

"Well, he's concerned," Lanham nodded. "He's definitely concerned with your future – just as he is with *my* future, and with the future of every man at M and D. He's that kind of guy."

The waitress returned with their coffees, and Sid Lanham said, "Thanks, doll."

The girl smiled mechanically and again moved away.

"Cream?" Lanham asked.

"Black," replied Billy.

"Guess that's how I should take mine," Sidney Lanham said, pouring the thick yellow cream and stirring it. "That way you get the real flavor. Gives your taste buds a chance to do some honest work."

Billy looked at his steaming cup. "So you had this talk with Mr. Allen about me," he said.

"Not exactly a *talk*. We were gassing about the department, about some of the new men and your name just naturally sprang up."

"Naturally."

Lanham raised his cup and gingerly swallowed some of the hot liquid. "Stuff can burn your tongue. You feel it for days. Kind of an itching sensation on the tip, like little needles." He sipped again, then continued. "Well, so Mr. Allen thinks you've got all kinds of unrealized potential."

Billy smiled. "And it's the unrealized part that bothers him?"

"Now, that remark – it's a perfect example of what's wrong with you," exclaimed Sid. "The negative meaning you draw from words. Not positive, *negative*. And that's deadly. You've got all kinds of natural talent. You're intelligent and neat and you've got a nice clean smile and you know how to dress – but those are surface qualities. Hell, Billy, you've also got to have a positive, aggressive attitude."

"Like you have, Sid?"

"Sure. I have it. And so did Mr. Allen when he was selling in the field. And so does Dave Markelson. All of the top boys have this kind of attitude. They're all *positive* people."

"Dave Markelson is a positive ass," said Billy.

"Forget Markelson," Lanham snapped, waving his hand. "Concentrate on what I'm saying. You've got to overhaul your attitude." Lanham swallowed more coffee. "For example, when you come into the office in the morning you ought to be mentally prepared for the day ahead. And, obviously, you're not."

"How do you mean, I'm not?"

"You arrive quiet and glum and you don't say much to any of us. And when Mr. Allen comes in you don't make any concrete, positive attempt to show him your spirit. He wants to believe that every man is a live wire, a go-getter, a doer. He wants to see spirit and bounce."

"And you, Sid, you always give it to him?"

"Damn right I do. I may feel like hell; I may have a stinking hangover from making the night spots with a customer, but I don't show it. I smile. I snap my fingers and let him know I'm ready to do a job. You must tell yourself mentally that you're going to give it everything you've got. Every day. You say to yourself, 'Today is going to be the *best* day I've ever had. I'm going to go out and really sell like crazy today!' My God. Billy, last Thursday I heard you tell Mr. Allen that things were slow. Things are *never* slow. Never! Not for a good salesman they aren't, because selling is a state of mind. You never even allow for the possibility that things are going to be slow."

Billy shrugged. "He asked me how things were, and I didn't see any point in lying. He's got the figures. July is our slowest month – so when he asked me I told him."

"Bad." Sidney Lanham shook his head. "Bad mistake. I

hope you can see that."

Billy sipped his coffee. It was getting cool.

"Take me," said Sidney Lanham, tapping his chest. "I never allow anything to get the best of me. In high school I was skinny and I got tired real easy. I hated exercise – but I told myself I should be doing pushups. I told myself I could do fifty pushups every afternoon in the gym – and by God, I *did* fifty pushups. Oh, not right away. By degrees, as my stomach muscles got stronger. Took me six months before I could do my fifty pushups. But I did it. Now my stomach is like a rock. Feel it, Billy – like a rock."

Billy poked at Sid Lanham's stomach.

"Like a rock," he agreed.

"Selling is the same way," Lanham went on, signaling the waitress for more coffee. "You tell yourself you're going to sell fifty units a week. First, it seems impossible, but you keep hammering away and then, by God, you're doing it!"

"Have you ever done it?"

"Done what?"

"Sold fifty units in one week?"

"Hell, no! Only Mr. Allen himself ever cracked fifty in one week at Moffitt and Dodson."

"Then why fool yourself?" Billy asked. "Selling even twenty-five units a week is something like a miracle. You have to–"

"Listen!" Sid cut in. "There are no miracles in the selling game. A salesman makes his own miracles. If Mr. Allen sold fifty units in his day then we can sell fifty units in ours."

"Things are different now."

"The point is, Billy, your mental outlook is crippling you. It's weak and negative when it should be strong and positive. You do want to stay in the selling game don't you?"

"I guess so," said Billy. "I've never really considered anything else. Dad was a salesman all his life."

"Your dad was one *hell* of a salesman. Moffitt and Dodson could use ten more just like him today."

The waitress brought over a fresh pot of coffee and filled their cups.

"Now," said Lanham stirring in the cream, "let's set up a plan."

"What kind of plan?"

"A concrete positive plan of action. When we go back to the office and Mr. Allen asks you how you're coming along, you say 'Great, just great!' and you smile and kind of stand up on the balls of your feet. Kind of springy and light. Mr. Allen likes to see pent-up energy in his men."

"I'm not sure I could do that," said Billy Spiker.

"Nonsense!" shouted Lanham, and the waitress at the counter looked up. "That's just another example of negative thinking. What if I'd given in to my stomach muscles back in high school, let them know I couldn't do my fifty pushups? Then what?"

Billy said nothing.

"You have to put on a front for Mr. Allen. That's only using common sense, isn't it?"

"Maybe," said Billy Spiker.

"You're on the M and D team, Billy," Lanham assured him, "and we're rooting for you. Every man at Moffitt and

Dodson wants to keep his company strong – and that means healthy competition."

"Well, I'm not going to offer much healthy competition with *my* territory. They handed me a lemon."

Lanham's face flushed; a vein pulsed in his temple.

"That's rotten talk! You're still new; you've got to *earn* a better territory. Hell, they stuck me on a rough run too, back in the beginning. But I just gritted my teeth and got in there and–"

"–and plugged."

"Right. I plugged. Goddam right I did. Later the breaks began to come my way, but I took it on the chin for a couple of years, That's the way we all start."

Billy looked intently at Sid Lanham. "I'm not the bounce-back-smiling type, Sid, and you may as well understand that. You and Mr. Allen and all the others. I hate childish lies and playing kids' games. If you believe in a product then you do your best to sell that product. It's that simple as far as I'm concerned. All this other rah-rah stuff is crap – and you know it. My God, Sid, you're forty-six and you try to act like you're twenty-one and just out of college around Allen." He leaned across the table. "Now. Let me ask *you* something. Just how fair has the company been to you?"

Lanham frowned. "Fair? Why – the company's always provided me and my family with a fine living."

"A living, Sid – not a *fine* living. You keep hoping to be put in charge of central sales, but you know and I know that they want a younger man. They want Dave Markelson. And unless you stand up to Allen, they're going to go right on pushing you around. Tell him you'll quit if you don't get that promotion, then see what he says."

"By God, I *should*," admitted Lanham. "You know, for a long while now, I've been telling myself, Sid, boy, you tell that snake Dave Markelson to go straight to hell next time you see him. Then you march into Allen's office and say your say."

"Fine. Do it, Sid. *Do* it."

Lanham spoke softly. "I will! I'll tell him what I want and I'll tell him that Dave Markelson is a crooked son of a bitch. Which he is."

"Definitely," said Billy Spiker. "A prime s.o.b."

Lanham finished his coffee and smiled. His eyes were shining. "Let's get back," he said.

They left enough change on the table to cover the tip and moved toward the exit. The glass doors opened and a tall, brisk-looking, crewcut young man stepped through.

"Afternoon, Spiker," he said to Billy. Then, to Sid: "Hi, Lanham. How goes it fella?"

Sidney Lanham hesitated for a long second. Then he seemed to rise up on the balls of his feet. "Great!" he said to Dave Markelson, smiling his practiced salesman's smile, "Just great, Dave!"

And he did not look at Billy Spiker during their long, silent walk back to the office.

SEVERAL OF THE BEST STORIES in this book took years to find a market. They didn't fit a commercial genre. Editors were afraid to buy them. However, just six months after I wrote "The Grackel Question," the story was in print. Why? Because it's science fiction. A safe genre with a ready audience.

This story is a prime example of what the late Theodore Sturgeon termed "the zany side" of my personality. The tale is openly wild and crazy. Nearly everything I have included in *Ships in the Night* is serious. Yet humor has always been a vital part of my life as man and writer. Therefore, this book would not be complete without a sample of it.

Yes, there is humor in "Helle on Wheels," but this story is the only totally mad piece in my collection. In "The Grackel Question" I pull out all the stops.

So sit back and get ready to meet my zany side.

And watch out for Grackels!

THE GRACKEL QUESTION

ARNOLD HASTERBROOK I, II, AND III was crossing the Greater Continental Federated United States for the sixteen-thousandth time in his customized hoverbug when he saw two lovely hitchies by the side of the road.

Really gorgeous ones. With twinkly breasts fully exposed, of course, and long, sunbuttered Texas legs.

Arnold hovered above them, leaning out of the podvent. "I hope you're not Grackels," he said.

Big teeth-and-gums smile from one. "Is that a question?"

"I'll *make* it a question," said Arnold. "Are you Grackels?"

"Yo," they said together, nodding and looking despondent. "But we didn't know it till now." (This from the first Grackel.)

That was the odd thing about a Grackel: when you asked it a direct question about its origin it *had* to tell you the truth. No lies. No evasions. The plain, unvarnished truth. And, sometimes, the host body didn't know it was a Grackel, until you asked, but it could never evade the question.

"Freeb you, fella!" the second Grackel said, giving him the elbow. "You've ruined *our* day."

"Sorry," muttered Arnold, and he was – but only for himself. If they'd been human, he would have been delighted to give them a hitch into New OldSanAntone. Two plush-breasted little teeny kids who'd do *anything* for a ride. He'd been sexed by a hitchie twice this trip, and it really twigged him off to pass these.

But pass them he must. Arnold had a marked distaste for Grackels; he just couldn't seem to adapt to them. And, at three hundred, he was too old to change his ways.

He sighed, reactivated his bug, and headed for New OldSanAntone.

Arnold Hasterbrook I, II, and III had a vexing problem; he was an Immortal. Born in 1879, the year Thomas Edison produced the first commercially practical incandescent lamp, he had lived long enough now to see most of the Greater Continental Federated United States infiltrated by Grackels.

Grackels could, of course, assume the shape of *any* living creature in *any* solar system. Earth was just one more apple in their barrel. They would land one of their repulsive jellyships in a remote spot, slither into town before dawn, and effortlessly absorb everything – cats, dogs, alligators, hippos, tree sloths, beetles, elephants, porcupines, worms, bees, birds, flies, bedbugs, and people. They were not at all selective. They'd take over anything, since they hated being regular Grackels. Anything was better than looking like putrid jello.

So damn many Grackels were around these days that folks had stopped asking them if they *were* Grackels. What freebing good did it do to find out? It was depressing to know, since there was nothing to be done about them. If you caught one in its natural state (*phew!*) before it infiltrated, you couldn't kill it. It would just split into more little Grackels. After awhile, people stopped trying.

It wasn't bad, living with them. If one absorbed a warthog, it acted thereafter exactly like a warthog. Another warthog, looking for companionship, wouldn't know the difference.

Same in regard to humans. As Youngos, they played vidball, climbed neartrees, yelled, and raised hell. As Midos, they watched the Trivid, drank NearBud, smoked NoTars, scratched their pot bellies, and argued local politics. As Oldos, they sat in the sun, played Cardchecks, and fell asleep after dinner. With plenty of sexing along the way. It felt just as good to sex a Grackel as it did a non-Grackel. No difference.

So who really gave a damn?

There was just one big drawback. They were killing Earth. A Grackel could not reproduce while inhabiting an alien body, so very few human babies were born these days. Ditto alligators and field mice – you name it. When the

body they were in died, the Grackel died with it. No rever-
sion.

Since there were an estimated ten billion trillion
Grackels within our galaxy, a few million dead ones each
month represented a mere dripple in the cosmic bucket.

So, if you were human, you adapted. But, to Arnold
Hasterbrook I, II, and III, it was not a simple matter of
adaptation. As an Immortal, he wished to procreate. He
wanted immortal sons and immortal daughters – and pairbonding with a Grackel just wouldn't get the job done.

Arnold was unique.

In December of 1879 an eccentric scientist in Des
Moines, Iowa – Dr. Ludwig O'Hallahan, of German-Irish
descent – discovered a serum which produced immortality
upon injection. He used this serum on a dozen newborn
infants – six males and six females – before his lab exploded (defective boiler). In the blast Dr. O'Hallahan was killed,
and his serum destroyed.

The twelve babies survived, being immortal, and were
returned to their parents.

There were no more immortal humans born after 1879.

Arnold had grown normally, unaware of his unique condition, cut off from all contact with the other eleven
Immortals. When he passed the age of 124 and did not look
a day over thirty-five, he knew he was special. Every mem-
ber of his family had died, including all five of his younger
brothers. (They died hating him because he had not gone
bald.)

Much earlier, when he was still a young man, Arnold

was contacted by Dr. O'Hallahan's fat wife (who had been baking gingerbread in the yard at the time of the explosion), and she told him, giggling, that he was an Immortal.

He thought about that fact for a hundred years – and, in March of 2004, began his search.

For an immortal woman.

There were six of them around, he knew – and Arnold only needed one.

Now it was Newjune of 2179, and he was still looking.

On the outskirts of New OldSanAntone, Arnold quick-parked his bug and entered a pubflush to drain his bladder.

"Wahoo!" said a robust robovoice as he did so. "Take your hat off to Texas!"

"I don't wear a hat," said Arnold. "Your scanplate must be defective."

And when he'd finished, the voice said robustly, "Ya'll come back an' see us now, ya hear."

Arnold went to the pubman. "You've got a defective urinal in there," he told the fellow.

"Freeb off!" growled the man.

Outside the pub, Arnold saw a woman and her babe near the femflush.

"Howdy," said Arnold, walking over to her. He looked down at her cribtot. "Cute."

"Just average," shrugged the woman.

"Bet he can talk! He *looks* like he can talk," said Arnold.

"At three months?" asked the woman.

"Youngos can surprise you sometimes," Arnold told her.

He hunkered down next to the tot. "Boopy, oopy, goopy," he said.

The infant gurgled, spitting up. "Satisfied?" asked the bored mother.

"I'm going to ask your child a question," Arnold said. He looked down at the tot. "Are you a Grackel?"

"I *shore* am, pard!" said the baby in a clear, robust voice. Arnold smiled.

The mother shrieked.

When Arnold popped back into his bug, he was still smiling. Somehow, he took a perverse pleasure in exposing Grackels. Damn slimy things! He didn't bother questioning many frogs or moths, but tots were a specialty of his. A lot of mothers across the length and breadth of the Greater Continental Federated United States despised Arnold Hasterbrook I, II, and III.

But that was all right. He'd exposed a lot of Grackels.

New OldSanAntone sparkled in the Texas sun. After the pesky red dust of the Badlands, Arnold found the city's soft green a refreshing change. He metered his bug at a pubpark, and he strolled for a pape. The usual routine.

In every new city Arnold scanned the local pape's "Personal" column. He hoped he might someday encounter a boxitem relating to immortality. It was a vague hope, and after 175 years he really didn't think his luck would change in New OldSanAntone.

He approached a dented robovendor. The machine held

a stack of papes in a weathered metal hand. It was motionless.

"I'll take one," said Arnold.

The machine said nothing.

Arnold reached out, gripped the edge of the top pape, and pulled.

"Whoa, now, *watch* it, cowpoke!" growled the machine. "You don't get a pape till I feel a silver Vegasbuck slide into my tummy!"

"Usually I receive and then I pay," protested Arnold.

"I reckon not in this town you don't, wrangler."

Irritated, Arnold unsnapped his waistpurse and took out a silver dollar.

"Sock it to me!" said the machine.

Arnold inserted the large square coin into the robot's slotted navel.

It giggled. "Always tickles going down!"

Arnold grabbed his pape and stalked off with it.

"Ya'll come back an' see us now," yelled the machine. "Ya hear?" Then it lapsed back into motionless silence.

Under "Personal," Arnold Hasterbrook I, II, and III was astonished to find the following item:

300-YEAR-OLD IMMORTAL WOMAN
WARM AND ATTRACTIVE
SEEKS IMMORTAL MAN
FOR PURPOSES OF PAIRBONDING
AND PROCREATION.
PUNCH 660-23

Arnold read it three times. There it was! In bold black and white: *the* ad. After 175 years! He was stunned, grinning like a Youngo at his first Fed-sponsored sexorg.

Quickly, Arnold moved to a pubvid, palmed for credit, then punched 66023. And waited, heart beating rapidly, his upper lip twitching (which it always did when he was excited).

The screen bloomed. A fem was there and she was, indeed, warm and attractive. She wore Globright on her nips. "Hello," she said.

"Hello," said Arnold.

"I'm Edwina," she said, smiling. "Edwina Murch."

"Ugly name," said Arnold.

"Yes, I've always *hated* it. Call me Ed."

"However, you are warm and attractive, Ed, and that's what counts. And I like your Globrights."

"Thanks," she said. "I *do* have perky nips and better-than-average buttocks."

"May I see your strawberry?"

"Of course," she replied, and uncovered her right shoulder. On the upper flesh a pink, strawberry-shaped mark was clearly visible.

"Now show me yours," she said. Arnold did that.

No doubt about it, they were both Immortals.

"My name is Arnold Fitzstephan Hasterbrook, First, Second, and Third," he told her. "And I'm three hundred years old."

"How lovely!"

"I suggest that we meet at a floatshop for a cof and some gab," said Arnold. "Comply?"

"Comply," she said. "Let's make it the Alamo in ten."

"Right," said Arnold. "In ten." And he punched out.

When Edwina Murch appeared exactly ten minutes later, she had a dog with her – a large St. Bernard on a sturdy, lifeleather leash. The beast lolled its wide pink tongue at Arnold. Its eyes were sleepy and bored.

"This is Ernest," she said. "Ernest, say hello to the nice gentleman."

"*Woof*," said Ernest, with a listless swish of his massive tail. Then he slumped heavily to the floor of the floatshop.

"Bet he puts away a lot of nearsteak," said Arnold.

She smiled, leaned to ruffle the beast's fur. "Actually, Ernest is rather finicky. Has a delicate digestive tract."

"I see," said Arnold. He looked around nervously. After 175 years he found it difficult to talk to women.

"Hey! Over *here*, folks!" a voicetable yelled at them. "I'm empty!"

"Shall we sit for a cof?" Arnold asked.

"By all means."

As she walked ahead of him to the table, Arnold could not help admiring her cunning buttocks. Definitely better than average. She wore the latest in disposable Slipsheer-Seethru femsuits. And her Globrights swayed as she walked. Arnold felt his upper lip twitching.

"Come on, Ernest, come, sweets!"

Ernest got up, shambled after them, collapsing at Edwina's dainty feet.

"Welcome, thrice welcome," said the table as they sat down. "Your robo will be here in a jiff!"

The view was spectacular.

They were floating a full mile above New OldSanAntone. In 2006, when Texas went bankrupt and the Vatican had purchased the State, the Alamo was leased to the GM-Cofburg Combine. They promptly had it converted into a deluxe, antigrav floatshop. The historic old Mission, originally a money-loser, was now a prime tourspot, notching a fat annual profit for GM-C.

Their robo cowwaiter, wearing stitched leather boots and a tall, white ten-gallon hat, rolled up to the table. "How y'all?" it asked robustly. "What'll it be today for you good folks? Got a mighty fine special on Texas closesteak smothered in nea-ronions. Real humdinger of a meal for fifty palmcreds!"

Arnold shook his head. "Just bring us two Santa Anas and a couple of cofs, with everything. Medium-well for me."

"Rare," said Edwina.

"–and rare for the lady."

"You bet. Yessireebob. Yahoo!" And the machine clicked, whirred, bowed and rolled briskly away, humming *Yellow Rose of Texas*.

"Friendly chap," Arnold observed. "I had a nasty run-in with a stubborn vending machine just before I punched you."

"I don't usually drink this early in the afternoon," smiled Edwina, "but today is a special occasion, wouldn't you say?"

"Oh, I certainly would say."

"Thought no one was *ever* going to answer my ad," she sighed.

Arnold was curious about her background. "You're not a native Texan, that's for sure," he said. "How'd you happen to end up out here in New OldSanAntone?"

"Bozie, my baby brother, got into artificial steer manure," she said. "They need a lot for the robo rodeos. Atmosphere, you know."

Arnold nodded.

"Well, we moved out here to Texas when I was a hundred and two. Bozie was eighty." She smiled. "Been here ever since. At least I have. When Bozie died – not being immortal – they shipped him back to Des Moines."

"There's good money in manure," said Arnold reflectively.

"And what do *you* do for a living?"

"I design bugs," he told her.

"You mean grasshoppers? Butterflies?"

"Hoverbugs. Design 'em and build 'em. Last year's Indy 1500 – one of my bugs won it. Fastest bug on the bowl."

"Fascinating," she said.

"Been at it a while," he told her. "Got into the game back in 1902 when I was a lot younger." He chuckled. "Worked for Henry Ford. I was what you might call a 'ghost designer' on his Model T. Ford didn't want to give me credit. Hank was funny that way."

"Fascinating," she said again.

"Uh, just when *did* you put your ad in the pape?" Arnold asked.

"The summer I turned a hundred and sixteen. Sweet one sixteen, and never been kissed. I guess you could say my juices were stirring." And she blushed, lowering her eyes.

"Fate took a hand in this," Arnold nodded. "We were *destined* to pair-bond. Don't you think I'm right, Ed?"

"Yes, I do, Arnie. Indeed I do!" The Santa Anas arrived, bubbling.

"Well, Ed," said Arnold, raising his nearglass. "Here's to the *next* three hundred years – of togetherness!" And he winked at her. Her shyness made him bolder.

"Oh, I don't know if I could spend three hundred years with the same man," she confessed.

"So what? So if we get bored, after a hundred years or thereabouts, we can detach. At least by then our kids will be grown." He took a large swallow of his drink. "How many should we have?"

Edwina blushed again. "You decide," she said in a small voice.

"Two immortal males, two immortal females," declared Arnold. "How does that sound?"

"Sounds fine," nodded Edwina, delicately sipping her Santa Ana.

"But first, right off, I have to ask you a question."

"Feel free," she said.

"Are you a Grackel?"

She blinked at him, shifted nervously in her slotseat.

"*Are* you?"

"Heavens, no!" she said, frowning. "Just the *thought* of it…" She shivered.

"Would you mind if I asked your dog the same question?"

"Ernest?"

"Yes," said Arnold. "I have to know. If he *is* one, then we can't keep him. I won't have one in the house."

136

"All right," she said. "Ask him."

"Ernest," said Arnold, meeting the dog's soulful gaze, "I'm going to ask you if you are a Grackel. If the answer is yes, bark once. If no, *twice*. Are you ready?"

Ernest regarded him sleepily, tongue lolling. He was ready.

"*Are* you a Grackel?"

"*Woof*," barked Ernest.

A long moment of tension followed. Then, lazily, "*Woof*."

"He *isn't* one!" cried Edwina in triumph, hugging the shaggy animal. His massive tail thumped the floor.

By then their cofburgers had arrived. Between bites, Arnold said, "Well, I guess that settles it."

"One final thing," said Edwina, chewing.

"What's that?"

"Are you a Grackel?"

Arnold Fitzstephan Hasterbrook I, II, and III was absolutely amazed to hear himself reply, "Yes, as a matter of fact, I *am*."

As a bachelor, his answer depressed him for the rest of his life.

Which was forever.

ONCE AGAIN, as in "Just Like Wild Bob," we encounter Barney Oldfield. The historic 1902 race at Grosse Pointe, Michigan, described in this narrative established Oldfield's career and helped launch the Ford Motor Company. But this is not a tale of automobile racing; this is a love story, a gentle excursion into period romance.

There is darkness here, and fantasy, but the primary ingredient is love, the deep bonding of two very different people from very different worlds.

"Of Time and Kathy Benedict" is from the heart.

OF TIME AND KATHY BENEDICT

NOW THAT SHE WAS ON THE LAKE, with the Michigan shore-line lost to her, and with the steady cat-purr of the outboard soothing her mind, she could think about the last year, examine it thread by thread like a dark tapestry.

Dark. That *was* the word for it. Three dark, miserable love affairs in twelve dark, miserable months. First, with Glenn, the self-obsessed painter from the Village who had worshiped her body but refused to consider the fact that a brain went with it. And Tony, the smooth number she'd met at the new Disco off Park Avenue, with his carefully tailored Italian suits and his neurotic need to dominate his women. Great dancer. Terrific lover. Lousy human being. And, finally, the wasted months with Rick, God's gift to architecture, who promised to name a bridge after her if she'd marry him and raise his kids – three of them from his last divorce. She had tried to make him understand that as an independent woman, with a going career in research, she wasn't ready for instant motherhood at twenty-one. And there was the night, three months into their relationship, when Rick drunkenly admitted he was bisexual and actually preferred males to females. He'd taken a cruel pleasure in explaining this preference to her, and that was the last time they'd seen each other. Which was…when? Over two months ago. Early October now, and they'd split in late July.

She looked ahead, at the wide, flat horizon of the lake as the small boat sliced cleanly through the glittering skin of water.

Wide. Timeless. Serene.

What had Hemingway called it? The last "free place." The sea. She smiled. Lake St. Clair wasn't exactly what he'd been talking about, but for her, at this moment, it would do just fine. She did feel free out here, alone on the water, with the cacophonous roar of New York no longer assaulting her mind and body. The magic peace of the lake surrounded her like a pulsing womb, feeding her hunger for solitude and silence. This assignment in Michigan had been a true blessing, offering her the chance to escape the ceaseless roar of the city.

"Dearborn? Where's that?"

"Where the museum is…in Detroit. You can check out everything at the museum. They've got the car there."

Her boss referred to "999" – the cumbersome, flat-bodied, tiller-steered vehicle designed by Henry Ford and first raced here at Grosse Pointe, just east of Detroit, late in

1902. The newspaper she worked for was planning a special feature piece celebrating the eighty-year anniversary of this historic event. Old 999 was the car that launched the Henry Ford Motor Company, leading to the mass-production American automobile.

"The museum people restored it, right down to the original red paint. It's supposed to look exactly like it did back in 1902," Kathy's boss had told her. "You go check it out, take some shots of it, dig up some fresh info, then spend a few days at Grosse Pointe...get the feel of the place."

She'd been delighted with the assignment. Autumn in Michigan. Lakes and rivers and hills... Trees all crimson and gold... Sun and clear blue sky... Into Detroit, out to the Henry Ford Museum in Dearborn, a look at Ford's birthplace, a long talk with the curator, some pictures of ridiculous old 999 ("...and they named her after the New York Central's record-breaking steam locomotive") and on out to Grosse Pointe and this lovely, lonely, soothing ride on the lake. Just what she'd been needing. Balm for the soul.

As a little girl, she'd vacationed with her parents in Missouri and Illinois, in country much like this – and the odors of crushed leaves, of clean water, of hills rioting in autumn colors came back to her sharply here on the lake. It was a reunion, a homecoming. Emotionally, she *belonged* here, not in the rush and rawness of New York. Maybe, she told herself, when I save enough I can come here to live, meet a man who loves lakes and hills and country air.

Something was wrong. Suddenly, disturbingly wrong.

The water was gradually darkening around the boat; she

looked up to see an ugly, bloated mass of gray-black clouds filling the lake sky. It seemed as if they had instantly materialized there. And, just as suddenly, a cold wind was chopping at her.

Kathy recalled the warning from the old man at the boathouse: "Wouldn't go too far out if I was you, miss. Storm can build up mighty fast on the lake. You get some mean ones this time of year. Small boat like this is no good in a storm…engine can flood out…lotsa things can go wrong."

The clouds rumbled – an ominous sound – and rain stung her upturned face. A patter at first, then heavier. The cold drops bit into her skin through her skirt and light sweater. Lucky thing she'd taken her raincoat along "just in case." Kathy quickly pulled the coat on, buttoning it against the wind-blown rain.

Time to head back, before the full storm hit. She swung the boat around toward shore, adjusting the throttle for maximum speed.

The motor abruptly sputtered and died. Too much gas. Damn! She jerked at the start rope. No luck. Again. And again. Wouldn't start. Forget it; she was never any good with engines. There were oars and she could row herself in. Shore wasn't far, and she could use the exercise. Good for her figure.

So row. Row, row, row your boat…

As a child, she'd loved rowing. Now she found it was tougher than she'd remembered. The water was heavy and thick; it seemed to resist the oars, and the boat moved sluggishly.

The storm was increasing in strength. Rain stabbed at

her, slashing against her face, and the wind slapped at the boat in ice-chilled gusts. God, but it was cold! Really, really cold. The coat offered no warmth; her whole body felt chilled, clammy.

Now the lake surface was erupting under the storm's steadily increasing velocity; the boat rocked and pitched violently. Kathy could still make out the broken shoreline through the curtaining rain as she labored at the oars, but it grew dimmer with each passing minute. Her efforts were futile: She was rowing *against* the wind, and whenever she paused for breath the shoreline fell back, with the wind forcing her out into the heart of the lake.

She felt compelled to raise her head, to scan the lake horizon. Something huge was out there. Absolutely monstrous! Coming for her. Rushing toward the boat.

A wave.

How could such a mountain of water exist here? This ravening mammoth belonged in Melville's wild sea – not here on a Michigan lake. Impossible, she told herself; I'm not really seeing it. An illusion, created by freak storm conditions, unreal as a desert mirage.

Then she heard the roar. Real. Horribly, undeniably real.

The wave exploded over her, a foam-flecked beast that tossed her up and over in its watery jaws – flinging her from the boat, taking her down into the churning depths of the lake.

Into blackness.

And silence.

"You all right, miss?"

"Wha – what?"

"I asked if you're all right. Are you hurt? Leg broken or anything? I could call a doctor."

She brought the wavering face above her into focus.

Male. Young. Intense blue eyes. Red hair. A nice, firm, handsome face.

"Well, ma'am, *should* I?"

"Should you what?" Her voice sounded alien to her.

"Call a doctor! I mean, you were unconscious when I found you, and I–"

"No. No doctor. I'm all right. Just a little…dizzy."

With his help, she got to her feet, swayed weakly against him. "Oops! I'm not too steady!"

He gripped her arm, supporting her. "I've gotcha, miss."

Kathy looked around. Beach. Nothing but water and beach. The sky was cloudless again as the sun rode down its western edge, into twilight. "Guess the storm's over."

"Beg your pardon, miss?"

"The wave…a really *big* one…must have carried me in." For the first time, she looked at this young man clearly – at his starched shirt with its detachable collar and cuffs, at his striped peg-top trousers and yellow straw hat.

"Are they doing a film here?"

"I don't follow you, miss."

She brushed sand from her hair. One sleeve of her raincoat was ripped, and her purse was missing. Gone with the boat. "Wow, I'm a real mess. Do I look terrible?"

"Oh…not at all," he stammered. "Fact is, you're as pretty as a Gibson Girl."

She giggled. "Well, I see that your compliments are in keeping with your attire. What's your name?"

"McGuire, ma'am," he said, removing his hat. "William Patrick McGuire. Folks call me Willy."

"Well, I'm Katherine Louise Benedict – and I give up. If you're *not* acting in a film here then what *are* you doing in that getup?"

"Getup?" He looked down at himself in confusion. "I don't–"

She snapped her fingers. "Ha! Got it! A party at the hotel! You're in *costume*!" She looked him over very carefully. "Lemme try and guess the year. Ummmm…turn of the century…ah, I'd guess 1902, *right*?"

Young McGuire was frowning. "I don't mean to be offensive, Miss Benedict, but what has this year to do with how I'm dressed?"

"*This* year?"

"You said 1902, and this *is* 1902."

She stared at him for a long moment. Then she spoke slowly and distinctly: "We *are* on the beach at Lake St. Clair, Grosse Pointe, Michigan, United States of America, right?"

"We sure as heck are."

"And what, exactly, is the month and the year?"

"It's October 1902," said Willy McGuire.

For another long moment Kathy didn't speak. Then, slowly, she turned her head toward the water, gazing out at the quiet lake. The surface was utterly calm.

She looked back at Willy. "That wave – the one that hit my boat – did you see it?"

"Afraid not, ma'am."

"What about the storm? Was anyone else caught in it?"

"Lake's been calm all day," said Willy, speaking softly. "Last storm we had out here was two weeks back."

She blinked at him.

"You positive *certain* you're all right, ma'am? I mean, when you fell here on the beach you could have hit your head…fall could have made you kinda dizzy and all."

She sighed. "I *do* feel a little dizzy. Maybe you'd better walk me back to the hotel."

What Kathy Benedict encountered as she reached the lobby of the Grosse Pointe Hotel was emotionally traumatic and impossible to deny. The truth of her situation was here in three-dimensional reality: the clip-clopping of horse-and-carriage traffic; women in wide feathered hats and pinch-waisted floor-length skirts; men in bowlers with canes and high-button shoes; a gaudy board-fence poster announcing the forthcoming Detroit appearance of Miss Lillian Russell – and the turn-of-the-century hotel itself, with its polished brass spittoons, ornate beveled mirrors, cut-velvet lobby furniture and massive wall portrait of a toothily grinning, walrus-moustached gentleman identified by a flag-draped plaque as "Theodore Roosevelt, President of the United States." She knew this was no movie set, no costume party.

There was no longer any doubt in her mind: The wave at Lake St. Clair had carried her backward eighty years, through a sea of time, to the beach at Grosse Pointe, 1902.

People were staring. Her clothes were alien.

Had she not been wearing her long raincoat she would have been considered downright indecent. As it was, she was definitely a curiosity standing beside Willy McGuire in the lobby of the hotel.

She touched Willy's shoulder. "I – need to lie down. I'm really very tired."

"There's a doctor in the hotel. Are you sure you don't want me to–"

"Yes, I'm sure," she said firmly. "But you *can* do something else for me."

"Just name it, Miss Benedict."

"In the water…I lost my purse. I've no money, Mr. McGuire. I'd like to borrow some. Until I can…get my bearings."

"Why, yes, of course. I surely do understand your plight." He took out his wallet, hesitated. "Uh…how much would be required?"

"Whatever you can spare. I'll pay you back as soon as I can."

Kathy knew that she'd have to find work – but just where did a 1982 female research specialist find a job in 1902?

Willy handed her a folded bill. "Hope this is enough. I'm a mechanic's helper, so I don't make a lot – an' payday's near a week off."

Kathy checked the amount. Ten dollars! How could she possibly do *anything* with ten dollars? She had to pay for a hotel room, buy new clothes, food… Then she broke into giggles, clapping a hand to her mouth to stop the laughter.

"Did I say something funny?" Willy looked confused.

"Oh no. No, I was just...thinking about the price of things."

He shook his head darkly. "Begging your pardon, Miss Benedict, but I don't see how *anybody* can laugh at today's prices. Do you know sirloin steak's shot up to twenty-four cents a pound? And bacon's up to twelve and a half! The papers are calling 'em 'Prices That Stagger Humanity!'"

Kathy nodded, stifling another giggle. "I know. It's absolutely frightful."

In preparing the Henry Ford story, she'd thoroughly researched this period in America – and now realized that Willy's ten dollars would actually go a long way in a year when coffee was a nickel a cup, when a turkey dinner cost twenty cents and a good hotel room could be had for under a dollar a night.

With relief, she thanked him, adding: "And I *will* pay it back very soon, Mr. McGuire!"

"Uh, no hurry. But...now that I've done you a favor, *I'd* like to ask one."

"Surely."

He twisted the straw hat nervously in his hands. "I'd mightily appreciate it – if you'd call me Willy."

It took her a long while to fall asleep that night. She kept telling herself: Believe it...it's real...it isn't a dream...you're really here...this is 1902...believe it, *believe* it, believe it...

Until she drifted into an exhausted sleep.

The next morning Kathy went shopping. At a "Come in

and Get to Know Us" sale in a new dry-goods store for ladies she purchased an ostrich-feather hat, full skirt, chemise, shoes, shirtwaist, and a corset – all for a total of six dollars and twenty-one cents.

Back in her hotel room she felt ridiculous (and more than a little breathless) as a hotel maid laced up her corset. But every decent woman wore one, and there was no way she could eliminate the damnable thing!

Finally, standing in front of the mirror, fully dressed from heels to hat, Kathy began to appreciate the style and feminine grace of this earlier American period. She had coiled her shining brown hair in a bun, pinning it under the wide-brimmed, plumed hat and now she turned to and fro, in a rustle of full skirts, marveling at her tiny cinched waist and full bosom.

"Kathy, girl," she said, smiling at her mirror-image, "with all due modesty, you are an *elegant* young lady!"

That same afternoon, answering a no-experience-required job ad for office help in downtown Detroit, she found herself in the offices of Dodd, Stitchley, Hanneford, and Leach, Attorneys at Law.

Kathy knew she could not afford to be choosy; right now, any job would do until she could adjust to this new world. Later, given her superior intelligence and natural talents, she could cast about for a suitable profession.

"Are you familiar with our needs, young lady?" asked the stout, matronly woman at the front desk. "Not really," said Kathy. "Your ad specified 'Office Help Female.'"

The woman nodded. "We need typewriters."

"Oh!" Kathy shrugged. "Maybe I copied the wrong address. I don't sell them."

"You don't sell what?" The woman leaned forward, staring at Kathy through tiny, square glasses.

"Typewriters," said Kathy. Suddenly she remembered that in 1902 typists were called "lady typewriters." There was so *much* to remember about this period!

"Frankly, miss, I do not understand what you are talking about." The buxom woman frowned behind her glasses. "*Can* you operate a letter-typing machine or can't you?"

"Yes, I can," nodded Kathy. "I really can." She smiled warmly. "And I *want* the job!"

Which is how Kathy Benedict, a $30,000-a-year research specialist from New York City, became an $8.00-per-week office worker with the firm of Dodd, Stitchley, Hanneford, and Leach in Detroit, Michigan, during October of 1902.

With her first week's pay in hand, Kathy marched up the steps of Mrs. O'Grady's rooming house on Elm Street and asked to see Mr. William McGuire.

"Why, Miss Benedict!" Willy seemed shocked to see her there in the hallway outside his room. He stood in the open door, blinking at her.

The left half of his face was covered with shaving cream.

"Hello, Willy," she said. "May I come in?"

"I don't think that would be proper. Not after dark and all. I mean, you are a single lady and these are bachelor rooms and it just isn't done!"

Kathy sighed. Again, she had failed to consider the period's strict rules of public conduct for unaccompanied females. She didn't want to cause Willy any embarrassment.

"Then could we meet downstairs...in the lobby?"

"Of course." He touched at his lathered cheek. "Soon as I finish shaving. I do it twice a day. Heavy beard if I don't."

"Fine," she said. "See you down there."

Waiting for Willy McGuire in the lobby of the Elm Street rooming house, Kathy reviewed the week in her mind. A sense of peace had entered her life; she felt cool and tranquil in this new existence. No television. No rock concerts. No disco. Life had the flavor of vintage wine. The panic and confusion of the first day here had given way to calm acceptance. She was taking this quaint, charming period on its own terms.

Willy joined her and they sat down on a high-backed red velvet couch. Willy looked fresh-scrubbed and glad to see her.

"Here's the first half of what I owe you," she told him, handing over the money. "I'll have the rest next week."

"I didn't expect any of it back this soon," he said.

"It was very kind of you to trust a stranger the way you did," Kathy smiled.

"I'd surely like to know you better, Miss Benedict. I hope we can be friends."

"Not if you keep calling me Miss Benedict."

"All right, then..." He grinned. "Kate."

"*Kate?*"

"Aye," said Willy. "Or would you prefer Katherine?"

"Nope. Kate will do fine. It's just that – nobody's called me that since I was six. Hmmmmm…" She nodded. "Willy and Kate. Has a certain *ring* to it!"

And, at that precise moment, looking at the handsome, red-haired young Irishman seated beside her, she realized that she had met a totally decent human being, full of warmth and honesty and manly virtue.

She decided to investigate the possibility of falling in love with him.

They rode in Willy's carriage through the quiet suburbs of Detroit that Sunday, savoring the briskness of the autumn air and the fire-colored woods. Sunlight rippled along the dark flanks of their slow-trotting horse and the faint sounds of a tinkling piano reached them from a passing farmhouse.

"I love horses," said Kathy. "I used to ride them all the time in Missouri."

"They're too slow for my taste," Willy declared. "I like to work with machines… Cycles, for instance. That's how I got started in this business. Bought me a motor-tandem last year. Filed down the cylinder, raised the compression, then piped the exhaust around the carburetor. She went like Billy Blue Blazes!"

"I don't much care for motorcycles. People get hurt on them."

"You can fall off a horse, too! Heck, I admit I've had me some spills on the two-wheelers, but nothin' serious. Hey – how'd you like to see where I work?"

"Love to," she said.

"Giddy-up, Teddy!" Willy ordered, snapping the reins. He grinned over at Kathy. "He's named after the President!"

Willy stopped the carriage in front of a small shop at 81 Park Place – where she was introduced to a gaunt, solemn-faced man named Ed "Spider" Huff.

"Spider's our chief mechanic, and I'm his assistant," Willy explained. "We work together here in the shop."

"On cycles?"

"Not hardly, ma'am," said Huff in a rasping, humorless voice. "This here is the age of the horseless carriage. Do you know we've already got almost two hundred miles of paved road in this country? In New York State alone, they got darn near a thousand automobiles registered."

"I assume, then, that you are working on automobiles?"

"We sure are," Huff replied. "But the plain truth of it is there ain't no other automobile anywhere on this whole round globe to match what we got inside – a real thoroughbred racing machine!"

"Spider's right for dang sure!" nodded Willy.

She was suddenly very curious. "Could I see it?"

Huff canted his head, squinting at her. He rubbed a gaunt hand slowly along his chin. "Wimminfolk don't cotton to racing automobiles. Too much noise. Smoke. Get grease on your dress."

"Truly, I'd *like* to see it."

Willy clapped Huff on the shoulder. "C'mon, Spider – she's a real good sport. Let's show her."

"All rightie," nodded Huff, "but I'll wager she won't favor it none." They led Kathy through the office to the shop's inner garage. A long bulked shape dominated the floor area, draped in an oil-spattered blanket.

"We keep her tucked in like a sweet babe when we ain't workin' on her," Willy declared.

"So I see," nodded Kathy.

"Well, dang it, Willy!" growled Huff. "If you're gonna show her, then *show* her!"

Willy peeled off the blanket. "There she is!" he said, with obvious pride in his tone.

Kathy stared at the big, square, red-painted racing machine, with its front-mounted radiator, nakedly exposed engine, and high, wire-spoked wheels. In place of a steering wheel an iron tiller bar with raised handgrips was installed for control – and the driver sat in an open bucket seat. There was no windshield or body paneling. "It's 999!" Kathy murmured. The two men blinked in shock.

"How'd *you* know we call her that?" Huff demanded.

"Uh…rumor's going around town that there's a racing car here in Detroit named after the New York Central's loco-motive. Some of the typewriters were talking about it at work."

"Good thing she's about ready to race," declared Willy. "Guess when you got a rig this fast word just leaks out."

"Anyway, it's a wonderful name for her. Who's the owner?"

"Our boss, Tom Cooper," said Huff. "Had a lot of trou-bles with 999 out at the track on the test runs an' old Hank

got fed up and sold out to Tom. They came into this as part-
ners – but Hank's out now."

"Hank?"

"Yeah," said Willy. "Hank Ford. Him an' Tom designed
her together."

"And not an extra pound of weight anywhere on 'er,"
said Huff. "That's why the engine's mounted on a stripped
chassis. She's got special cast-iron cylinder walls, giving a
seven-inch bore and stroke. And that, ma'am, is *power*!"

"Yep," nodded Willy. "She's the biggest four-cylinder rig
in the States. Separate exhaust pipes for each cylinder. We
can squeeze upward of seventy horse out of her! That
means, with the throttle wide open, on a watered-down
track, she'll do close to a mile a minute – better'n *fifty* miles
an hour!"

Kathy was excited; her assignment to research a race
eighty years in the past had become a present-day reality. "And
you've entered her against Alex Winton for the Manufacturers'
Challenge Cup at Grosse Pointe on October 25!"

They both stared at her.

"But how–" Willy began.

"Rumor," she added quickly. "That's the rumor I heard."

"Well, you heard right," declared Huff. "Ole Alex
Winton thinks that Bullet of his can't be beat. Him with his
big money and his fancy reputation. He's got a surprise
comin' right enough!"

Kathy smiled. "Indeed he has, Mr. Huff. Indeed he has."

Each afternoon after work Kathy began dropping by the

shop on Park Place to watch the preparations on 999. She was introduced to the car's owner, Tom Cooper – and to a brash, dark-haired young man from Ohio named Barney, an ex-bicycle racer who had been hired to tame the big red racing machine.

Of course she recognized him instantly, since he was destined to become as legendary as 999 itself. His full name was Berna Eli "Barney" Oldfield, the barnstorming daredevil whose racing escapades on the dirt tracks of America would earn him more fame and glory than any driver of his era. In March of 1910, at Daytona Beach, he would become the official "Speed King of the World" by driving a "Lightning" Benz for a new land speed record of 131 miles per hour. But here, in this moment in time, he was just a raw-looking twenty-four-year-old youth on the verge of his first automobile race. Kathy asked him if he smoked cigars.

"No, ma'am, I don't," said Oldfield.

And the next day she brought him one. He looked confused; ladies didn't offer cigars to gentlemen.

"Barney," she said. "I want you to have this for the race. It's important."

"But I told you, ma'am, I don't smoke cheroots!"

"You don't have to smoke it, just use it."

"You've lost me, ma'am."

"Horse tracks are bumpy, full of ruts and potholes. A cigar between your teeth will act to cushion the road shocks. Just do me a personal favor…try it!"

Oldfield slipped the fat, five-cent cigar into his coverall pocket. "I'll try it, Miss Benedict, because when a pretty lady asks me a favor I don't say no."

Kathy felt a current of excitement shiver along her body. When she'd been researching Oldfield, as part of her 999 assignment, she had difficulty in tracing the origin of Barney's cigar, his famed trademark during the course of his racing career. Finally, she'd uncovered an interview with Oldfield, given a month before his death in 1946, in which a reporter had asked: "Just where *did* you get your first cigar?"

And Barney had replied: "From a lady I met just prior to my first race. But I'll tell you the truth, son – I don't recall her name."

Kathy now realized that she was the woman whose name Barney had long since forgotten. The unique image of Barney Oldfield, hunched over a racing wheel, a cigar clenched between his teeth, began with Kathy Benedict.

They arrived at the Grosse Pointe track on Friday, October 24, a full day before the race, for test runs: Willy, Spider Huff, Cooper, and Oldfield. Kathy had taken sick leave from the office to be with them.

"We'll need all the practice time we can get," Willy told her. "Still some bugs to get out."

"McGuire!" yelled Tom Cooper. "You gonna stand there all day gabbin' your fool head off – or are you gonna crank her up? Now, *jump!*"

And Willy jumped.

Cooper was a square-bodied, gruff-looking man wearing a fleece-lined jacket over a plaid cowboy shirt – and he had made it clear that he didn't think women belonged around racing cars. Privately, Cooper had told Willy that he felt Kate Benedict would bring them bad luck in the race, but that he'd let her hang around so long as she "kept her place" and stayed out of their way.

Tom Cooper had always had strong ideas about what a "good woman" should be: "She ought to be a first-rate cook, be able to sing and play the piano, know how to raise kids and take care of a house, mind her manners, dress cleanly, be able to milk cows, feed chickens, tend the garden — know how to shop, be able to sew and knit, churn butter, make cheese, pickle cucumbers and drive cattle."

He had ended this incredible list with a question: "And just how many of these talents do *you* possess, Miss Benedict?"

She lifted her chin, looking him squarely in the eye. "The only thing I'm really good at, Mr. Cooper, is independent thinking."

Then she'd turned on her heel and stalked away.

In practice around the mile dirt oval, Barney found that 999 was a savage beast to handle at anything approaching full throttle.

"She's got the power, all right, but she's wild," he said after several runs. "Open her up and she goes for the fence. Dunno if I can keep her on the track."

"Are you willing to try?" asked Cooper. "You'll have to do better than fifty out there tomorrow to beat Winton's Bullet. Can you handle her at that speed?"

Oldfield squinted down from his seat behind the tiller. "Well," he grinned, "this damn chariot may kill me – but they will have to say afterward that I was goin' like hell when she took me through the rail!" He looked down sheepishly at Kathy: "And I beg yer pardon for my crude way of expression."

The morning of October 25, 1902, dawned chill and gray, and by noon a gust of wind-driven rain had dampened the Grosse Pointe oval. The popular horse track had originally been laid out over a stretch of low-lying marshland bordering the Detroit River, and many a spirited thoroughbred had galloped its dusty surface. On this particular afternoon, however, the crowd of two thousand excited citizens had come to see horsepower instead of horses, as a group of odd-looking machines lined up behind the starting tape. Alexander Winton, the millionaire founder of the Winton Motor Carriage Company and the man credited with the first commercial sale of an auto in the United States in 1898, was the odds-on favorite in his swift, flat-bodied Winton Bullet. Dapper and handsomely moustached, he waved a white-gloved hand to the crowd. They responded with cheers and encouragement: "Go get 'em, Alex!"

Winton's main competition was expected to come from the powerful Geneva Steamer, Detroit's largest car, with its wide wheelbase, four massive boilers, and tall stack – looking more like a landbound ship than a racing automobile. A Winton Pup, a White Steamer, and young Oldfield at the tiller of 999 filled out the five-car field.

Kathy spotted Henry Ford among the spectators in the main grandstand, looking tense and apprehensive; Ford was no longer the legal owner of 999, but the car *had* been built to his design, and he was anxious to see it win. In 1902, Ford was thirty-nine, with his whole legendary career as the nation's auto king ahead of him. His empire was still a dream.

Kathy's heart was pounding; she felt flushed, almost dizzy with excitement. The race she'd spent weeks reading about was actually going to happen in front of her; she was a vital, breathing part of the history she'd so carefully researched. At the starting line, she overheard Tom Cooper's last-minute words to Oldfield.

"All the money's on Winton," he was saying. "But we're betting you can whup him! What do you say, lad?"

"I say let him eat my dust. Nobody's gonna catch me out there on that track today."

"Do you think he can do it, Kate?" asked Willy, gripping her elbow as they stood close to the fence. "Do you think Barney can beat Winton? The Bullet's won a lot of races!"

"We'll just have to wait and see," she said, with a twinkle in her eyes. "But I can guarantee one thing – this race will go down in history!"

At the drop of the starter's flag all five cars surged forward, the high, whistling kettle-boil scream of the steamers drowned by the thunder-pistoned roar of 999 and the Winton Bullet.

Sliding wide as he throttled the bouncing red hell

wagon around the first turn, Barney immediately took the lead away from Winton. But could he *hold* it?

"Winton's a fox!" declared Willy as they watched the cars roar into the back stretch. "He's given Barney some room just to find out what 999 can do. See! He's starting his move now!"

Which was true. It was a five-mile event, and by the end of the first mile Alex Winton had Oldfield firmly in his sights, and was closing steadily with the Bullet as the two steamers and the Pup dropped back. It was a two-car race.

Barney knew he was in trouble. He was getting a continuous oil bath from the exposed crankshaft, and almost lost control as his goggles filmed with oil. He pushed them up on his forehead, knowing they were useless. But there was a greater problem: Bouncing over the ruts and deep-gouged potholes, the car's rigid ashwood-and-steel chassis was giving Oldfield a terrible pounding, and he was losing the sharp edge of concentration needed to win. On some of the rougher sections of the track the entire car became airborne.

Watching the Bullet's relentless progress, as Winton closed the gap between himself and Oldfield, Kathy experienced a sharp sense of frustration. At this rate, within another mile the Bullet would overhaul 999 and take the lead.

But that must not happen, she told herself. It *could* not happen. The pattern of the race was already fixed in history! Suddenly, she had the answer. "He forgot it!" she yelled to Willy.

"Forgot what?"

"Never mind! Just wait here. I'll be back."

And she pushed through the spectators, knocking off a fat man's bowler and dislodging several straw boaters; she had a destination and there was no time to waste in getting there.

When Oldfield neared the far turn, at the end of the back stretch, each new wheel hole in the track's surface rattling his teeth, he saw Kathy Benedict straddling the fence.

She was waving him closer to the rail, pointing to something in her hand, yelling at him, her voice without sound in the Gatling-gun roar of 999's engine.

Closer. And yet closer. What in the devil's name did this mad girl want with him?

Then she tossed something – and he caught it. By damn! The cigar!

It was *just* what he needed – and he jammed the cushioning cheroot between his teeth, lowered his body over the iron control bar, and opened the throttle. In a whirling plume of yellow dust, 999 hurtled forward.

Now let ole Winton try and catch him!

"Look at that!" shouted Willy when Kathy was back with him at the fence. "He's pullin' away!"

Oldfield was driving brilliantly now, throwing the big red wagon into each turn with fearless energy, sliding wide, almost clipping the fence, yet maintaining that hairline edge of control at the tiller. The blast from the red car's four open exhausts was deafening – and the crowd cheered wildly as 999 whipped past the main grandstand in a crimson blur.

By the third mile, Alex Winton was out, his over-strained

engine misfiring as the Bullet slowed to a crawl in Barney's dust.

And when Oldfield boomed under the finish flag, to a sea of cheering from the stands, he had lapped the second-place Geneva Steamer and left the other competitors far, far behind.

Willy jumped up and down, hugged Kathy, lifting her from the ground and spinning her in a circle, yelling out his delight.

Sure enough, just as she'd promised it would be, this one had been a race for the history books.

The morning papers proclaimed 999's triumph in bold black headlines: WINTON LOSES! OLDFIELD WINS! And the lurid copy described Barney as "hatless, his long, tawny hair flying out behind him with the speed of his mount, seeming a dozen times on the verge of capsize, he became a human comet behind the tiller of his incredible machine."

Reporters asked Barney what it was like to travel at a truly astonishing fifty miles per hour! How could mortal man stand the bullet-like speed?

Oldfield was quoted in detail: "You have every sensation of being hurled through space. The machine is throbbing under you with its cylinders beating a drummer's tattoo, and the air tears past you in a gale. In its maddening dash through the swirling dust the machine takes on the attributes of a sentient thing… I tell you, gentlemen, no man can drive faster and live!"

Henry Ford was quick to claim credit for the design and manufacture of 999, and the nation's papers headlined his name next to Oldfield's, touting the victory at Grosse Pointe as "the real beginning of the Auto Age."

Within a month, riding the crest of public acclaim, Hank Ford laid the foundations for his Ford Motor Company – already planning for the day when his "tin lizzies" would swarm the highways of America.

The victory of 999 also benefited Willy McGuire. "I want you and Spider to work for me from now on, Willy," Hank Ford had told him. "Cooper just doesn't appreciate you. And, for a start, I'll *double* your salary!"

During the days following the race at Grosse Pointe, Kathy fell deeply in love with the happy, red-haired Irishman. He was totally unlike any man she'd ever known: honest, kind, strong, gentle and attentive. And he loved her as a *complete* woman – mind and body. For the first time in her life, she had found real emotional fulfillment. His question was inevitable: "Will you marry me, Kate?"

And her reply came instantly: "Yes, yes, yes! Oh, yes, Willy, I'll marry you!"

As they embraced, holding one another tightly, Kathy knew that she was no longer afraid of anything. The old life was gone.

"Nothing frightens me now that I'm with you," she told him.

"Not even the lake?" he suddenly asked, his blue eyes intense.

She was startled by the question. "I never said that I was afraid of the lake."

"It's been obvious. We do everything together.

Ride…skate…picnic…attend band concerts. But you never want to go boating with me on the lake."

"I don't like boating. I told you that."

His eyes were steady on hers. "Then why were you on the lake alone the day I found you? What made you go out there?"

She sighed, lowering her eyes. "It's a long, long story and someday, when I'm sure you'll understand, I'll tell you all about it. I swear I will."

"It's a fine day, Kate. Sky's clear. No wind. No clouds. I think we ought to go out on the lake. Together."

"But why?"

"To put that final fear of yours to rest. It's like climbing back on a horse once he's bucked you off. If you don't, you never ride again. The fear is always there."

A strained moment of silence.

"I'm *not* afraid of the lake, Willy," she said in a measured tone.

"Then prove you're not! Today. Now. Show me, Kate!"

And she agreed. There was nothing to fear out there on the quiet water. She kept telling herself that over and over… Nothing to fear. Nothing. Nothing. Nothing.

The weather was ideal for boating – and Willy handled the oars with practiced ease, giving Kathy a sense of confidence and serenity.

She *did* feel serene out here on the placid lake. She enjoyed the pleasant warmth of the afternoon sun on her shoulders as she twirled the bright red parasol Willy had bought her just for this occasion.

The water was spangled with moving patterns of sun-light, glittering diamond shapes, shifting and breaking and re-forming in complex designs around the boat as Willy rowed steadily away from the shore.

In this calming aura of peace and natural beauty she wondered why she had been so afraid of the lake. It was lovely here, and there was certainly nothing to fear. The bizarre circumstances of that fateful afternoon in 1982 were unique; a freak storm had created some kind of time gate through which she had passed. And no harm had been done to her. In fact, she was grateful for the experience; it had brought her across a bridge of years to the one man she could truly love and respect.

She reached out to touch his shoulder gently. "Mr. McGuire, I love you."

He grinned at her. "And I love *you*, Miss Benedict!"

Willy laid aside the oars to take her into his arms. They stretched out next to one another in the bottom of the easy-drifting boat. The sky above them was a delicate shade of pastel blue (like Willy's eyes, she thought) and a faint breeze carried the perfume of deep woods out onto the water.

"It's an absolutely perfect moment," she said. "I wish we could put it in a bottle and open it whenever we get sad!"

"Don't need to," said Willy softly. "We've got a lifetime of perfect moments ahead of us, Kate."

"No." She shook her head. "Life is never perfect."

"*Ours* will be," he said, running a finger along the side of her sun-warm cheek, tracing the curve of her chin. "I'll make it perfect – and that's a promise."

She kissed him, pressing her lips deeply into his.

He sat up.

"Hey," she protested, opening her eyes. "Where'd you go? We were just getting started." And she giggled.

"Sky's darkening," he said, looking upward, shading his eyes. "I'd better row us in. A lake storm can–"

"*Storm!*" She sat up abruptly, staring at him, at the sky and water. "No! Oh, God, no!"

"Whoa there, you're shaking!" he said, holding her. "There's nothing to get worried over. We'll be back on shore in a few minutes."

"But you weren't *there*...you don't understand!" she said, a desperate tone in her voice. "That's just how the other storm came along – out of nowhere. And the wind..."

It was there, suddenly whipping at the lake surface.

He was rowing strongly now, with the boat cutting toward the shoreline. "Be on the beach in a jiffy. You'll see. Trust me, Kate."

But the wind was building rapidly, blowing against them, neutralizing Willy's efforts.

Kathy looked fearfully at the sky. Yes, there they were, the same ugly mass of gray-black clouds.

It began to rain.

"Hurry, Willy! Row faster!"

"I'm trying...but this wind's really strong!"

She sat in a huddled position in the stern of the boat, head down now, hands locked around her legs as the rain struck at her in blown gusts.

"Never seen a storm build up this fast," Willy grunted, rowing harder. "Freak weather, that's for sure."

How could he understand that she'd seen it all before, in a world eighty years beyond him? Clouds, wind, rain and–

And…

She knew when she looked up, slowly raising her head, that it would be there, at the horizon, coming for them.

The wave.

Willy stopped rowing at her scream. He looked toward the horizon. "God A'mighty!"

Then, in the blink of a cat's eye, it was upon them – blasting their senses, an angry, falling mountain of rushing water that split their boat asunder and pitched them into the seething depths of the lake.

Into blackness.

And silence.

Kathy opened her eyes.

She was alone on the beach. Somehow, without any visible proof, she knew she had returned to 1982.

And Willy was gone.

The thought tore through her, knife-sharp, filling her with desperate anguish.

Willy was gone!

She had lost him to the lake. It had given him to her and now it had taken him away.

Forever.

A husky lifeguard in orange swim trunks was running

toward her across the sand.

I don't *want* to be saved, she told herself; I want to go back into the lake and die there, as Willy had died. There's no reason to go on living. No reason at all.

"You all right, miss?"

Same words! Same voice!

She looked up – into the face of her beloved. The blue eyes. The red hair. The gentle, intense features.

"Willy!" she cried, suddenly hugging him. "Oh, God, Willy, I thought I'd lost you! I thought you were–"

She hesitated as the young man pulled back.

"Afraid you've made a mistake," he said. "My name's Tom."

She stared at him, and then she knew who he was. No doubt of it. Kathy *knew*.

"What about your middle name?"

"It's William," he told her. And then grinned. "Oh, I see what you mean – but nobody ever calls me Willy. Not since I was a kid."

"I know your last name," she said softly.

"Huh?"

"It's McGuire."

He blinked at her. "Yeah. Yeah, it is."

"Thomas William McGuire," she said, smiling at him. "Please…sit down here, next to me."

With a small sigh, he did so. She intrigued him. "When were you born?"

"In 1960."

"And who was your father? What was *his* name?"

"Timothy McGuire."

"Born?… The year?"

"My Dad was born in 1929."

"And your grandfather… What was *his* name and when was he born?"

"Patrick McGuire. Born in 1904."

Kathy's eyes were shining. She blinked back the wetness. "And his father, your great-grandfather–"

He started to speak, but she touched his lips with a finger to stop the words.

"He was William Patrick McGuire," she said, "and he was born in 1880, right?"

The young man was amazed. He nodded slowly. "Yeah. Right."

"And he survived a boating accident late in 1902, on *this* lake, didn't he?"

"He sure did, miss."

"Who was your great-grandmother?" Kathy asked.

"Her name was Patricia Hennessey. They met after the accident, that Christmas. They say he kind of–"

"Kind of what?"

"Kind of married her on the rebound. Seems he lost the girl he was going to marry in the boating accident. My great-grandma was what I guess you'd call a second choice."

Then he grinned (Willy's grin!), shaking his head. "I just can't figure how you knew about him… Are you a friend of the family?"

"No." She shook her head.

"And we've never met before, have we?"

She looked into the deep lake-blue of his eyes. "No, Willy, we've never met." She smiled. "But we're going to be friends…very, very good friends."

And she kissed him gently, softly, under the serene sky of a sun-bright Michigan afternoon on the shore of a placid lake in the autumn of a very special year.

HEREWITH, A STORY OF BARNSTORMING set in the 1920s, shortly after the First World War. I wrote it out of my boy-hood fascination with bi-planes ("two-wingers" as we called them back in Kansas City). I had a particular fondness for the JN-4, the old wood-and-canvas "Jenny" favored at coun-ty fairs by barnstorming stunt fliers. Clumsy, dangerous, yet romantically graceful, the Jenny made aviation history in the Roaring Twenties.

When I finished "The Sky Gypsy" I had nowhere to send it. Strictly non-genre. It sat in my files for more than two-and-a-half decades (yes, twenty-seven years!) before reach-ing print in a mainstream anthology published by Lord John Press in 1988. It later appeared on the Internet (without my permission) as "a classic of the sky."

I believe that this story is one of my very best. After reading it, I hope you'll share this view.

THE SKY GYPSY

THE BUZZING, FAINT AT FIRST, then growing louder to fill the sky, awakened Pres Thompson. He had been dozing in the shade of the Jenny, immersed in a kind of half-sleep in which he had mentally reflown the miles from Georgia, up through the South, then along the Gulf coast here into Texas, with the vast prairie land rolling away beneath his wings like an endless gray-green rug…

The sound in the sky brought him to his feet, and he peered upward, shading his eyes against the glare of Texas sun. In the bright arch of blue a graceful black-and-gold bird rode the upper currents, circling easily above him in great lazy swoopings.

"Haaaa-ay!" Pres shouted, waving his leather flying jacket.

The bird dipped its wings in salute.

It's the Solitaire! Pres told himself, running out to wave in the plane. *What a lucky break*!

177

The black-and-gold craft touched smoothly down, dust unraveling behind the tail skid as it taxied toward Pres. The blurring prop snapped to a standstill and the pilot slid over the edge of the cockpit to the ground. He was a tall man, well over six feet, and the sun flashed fire from his polished boots and felt-lined goggles. His smoke-colored flying jacket seemed tailored to fit his wide chest, and beneath a leather helmet of gold his face was long-boned, vulpine, the eyes dark and weathered along the cheek line. He walked forward, unknotting a white silk scarf at his neck.

"You got trouble, boy?" he asked.

"Not really," Pres admitted. "I am a little short on gas, but that's not the reason I waved you down." He paused, flushing. "I – I just wanted to meet you…"

The tall man grinned, shaking Thompson's hand. "Then you know who I am?"

"I *guess*!" nodded Pres. "For seven years – ever since I was twelve – I been hearing about you, Mr. Curry. I guess there's no man who flies don't know your name."

"I wouldn't go that far," said Stuart Nelson Curry. He lit a cigarette as Pres slowly circled the plane, now silent in the prairie heat except for the small metallic noises made by the cooling engine. The black wings, with the word SOLITAIRE lettered across the top, provided a sharp contrast against the gold fuselage, and the fabric was drum-tight and spotless.

"She's a real beauty," Pres sighed. "I've only seen one other Hisso Standard, and that was in Georgia where I picked up my ole Jenny. But it sure wasn't in *this* condition! What horsepower she give you?"

"Well, the Hispano is rated at one-fifty," said Curry, "but I coaxed thirty more out of this one. Did a few things to her."

"My crate's got the regular Curtiss," said Thompson, swinging his head in the direction of a battered JN-4, its wings tied down, at the edge of the clearing. "I'm lucky to get ninety horses out of her."

"Let's have a look," said Curry.

"She's a little beat up," said Pres, walking a step behind the taller man as they crossed the patch of hard ground. Thompson noted that the Solitaire walked with a slight limp. "I just got her last month. Guy only charged me four hundred, cuz she needed work. I patched the wings, put on a coat of dope and fixed up one of the wheels."

He kept on talking as Curry examined the plane.

"She still needs a few things, but the engine's okay. Runs fine with the new plugs."

Curry tapped the wing fabric with an index finger. "Loose," he said. "Could give you a bad time."

"I'll have 'em recovered when I can afford to," said Pres. "Right now I just want to make some money barnstorming. I'm aimed for the fair, up to Dorado. Then I guess I'll head on into Minnesota and follow out the season there. If I can make enough this summer I can really fix her up. Maybe even trade her for a Canuck."

Curry rubbed one hand thoughtfully along his jaw.

"Ever do any stunting?" he asked.

"Sure." Pres hesitated. "Well – I mean, not for money. I've put her through the usual stuff to get the hang of it. She stalls easy if you're not watching close, but she'll loop okay."

"I'm gonna tell you something, kid, and I think you better listen. This heap of yours is a death trap. In any kind of real dive those wings'll fold up like paper. Stunting isn't the cinch you make out, and that's one reason there are so damn many young fliers buried these days."

Curry's dark eyes were hard as they raked Thomson's face. Pres had a sudden mental picture of how it must have been, back in '18 on the Front, when Curry had a Hun in his sights. His eyes must have been hard then too, before the kill.

"She's tougher than you think," Pres said. "She'll stay pasted together unless I fly her like an idiot – which I don't plan to do."

Stuart Curry sighed, slapping his helmet against the leg of his gray cavalry pants. "Got any food with you?"

"Ham sandwiches," said Pres, "and a canteen of water. That do?"

"Fine. I was planning to put down for lunch. I'll share yours if you don't object."

"My pleasure," said Pres, feeling awkward and schoolboyish around Curry. Well, when you meet a man you've idolized, that's natural, and Stuart Nelson Curry was certainly an idol to a lot of people. In the war he'd earned his nickname, The Solitaire, because he flew so many solo missions against orders. Among the U.S. aces, only Rickenbacker had killed more Huns, and Curry might have beaten Rick if he'd reached the Front a little earlier.

They stretched out in the shade of a wing, eating quietly. Curry finished his sandwich, carefully wiped his hands on a large white handkerchief, then lay back, arms cradling his head.

"Me, I'm almost thirty," he said, "and already I'm an old man in this game. A kid your age ought to listen to what an old man tells him."

Pres said nothing, knowing Curry would continue.

"Let's say I was nineteen again, like you. What would I do? Would I take up some old boat with the wings peeling off and kill myself barnstorming for pork and bean money above a grandstand full of hicks?" Curry shifted position, leaning on one elbow, regarding Pres with a dark, steady gaze. "Kid, those lousy savages don't give a damn about you. They pay to see you split yourself open like a melon. They want to watch that Jenny of yours splatter all over the fairground, so they can rush out and strip it for souvenirs. And you along with it. I saw what the bastards did to Banty Rogers in Sioux City when he clipped a power line and rolled his Standard into a ball. They picked it clean as a bone – and when I finally got over to Banty – busting a few heads on the way – even his *socks* were gone. They just left his blood to cover him. That's all, just his blood…"

Pres watched a jaw muscle twitch in Curry's face.

"Why do you think I fly the best?" the tall man asked. "Because I don't want to give those human vultures a chance to get at me. I go on stunting because that's all a man like me can do – not because it's glamorous, or because they pay me more than any barnstormer in the business. I've seen it all. Nebraska, Kansas, Colorado – and it's the same dirty job. But at least it's flying – so I stunt. But a kid like you, at nineteen…"

"What *about* a kid like me?" asked Pres.

"You could get out before the game kills you. You could join the Flying Corp as a cadet and fly the latest – a DH with four hundred horses working for you, and no patched wings to worry about. That haywagon of yours won't do seventy, but a DH can crack one twenty-five. In a year, with some luck, you could graduate with a lieutenant's commission."

"Suppose I *like* being on my own, flying where I want to fly?" asked Thompson. "Suppose I become a good stunt pilot, even a great one – like you?"

"And suppose you break your fool neck trying to pull out of a spin next Sunday in Dorado?"

Pres Thompson leaned forward, chin against his knees. He stared at a clump of sage. "I'll take my chances," he said, "the way you took yours on the Front."

"That was war," Curry snapped, "and it didn't much matter whether you lived or died. I played Hero, and ended up with a plate in my leg and a hatful of tin medals. Now I'm a sky gypsy, with no home, no family, no future. Is that what you want out of life? Are you that dumb, kid, are you really *that* dumb?"

"I'm stunting at Dorado," said Thompson flatly. He got to his feet, pulling helmet and goggles from his scuffed leather jacket. "Will I see you there?"

"Dammit," snorted Curry, shaking his head. "If I had any sense I'd tell you to go to hell, but I've seen too many crashes. So I'll make a deal with you."

"Deal?" asked Pres, confused and a bit suspicious.

"What kind of deal?"

"Since you're determined to stunt that underpowered coffin I can use you in my act. I'm picking up my wing walker just this side of Dorado. Name's Slim Toulmin, and when he's sober he can do anything, short of hanging by his eyelashes. With Slim doing most of the wing stuff, then chuting down for the windup, and me taking on the high speed trick stuff with my Hisso, that leaves some easy bits for you – wingovers, banks, spirals and maybe a loop or two. I guess your cracker box can stand up under those. We'll split sixty-forty on the take. That way you get a taste of stunting, and I don't have to watch you turn yourself into a corpse. Fair enough?"

"Darn right, Mr. Curry!" Pres said, the delight showing in his smile.

"All right, we've got a deal. Now you can give me a hand with that prop."

And Stuart Nelson Curry moved away, limping across the clearing toward the waiting Standard.

"Ladeeez and gennelmen, the management of the Dorado County Fair proudly presents its star attraction, that inter-nationally famous war hero and daredevil sky king whose death-defying exploits have thrilled the world…"

The barker's deep voice continued to boom through the megaphone as Stuart Curry pulled the strap of his helmet tight and adjusted his goggles. He flicked a thumb in the direction of Thompson's Jenny.

"Better shake it, kid, we're up next."

A rising wave of cheers broke from the grandstand as Pres climbed into the cockpit of his JN, but he knew the acclaim was not for him; it belonged to the Solitaire. But if Pres did well up there today with the old Jenny then perhaps next week, next month, they'd be cheering for *him*…

The prop blurred into motion as the engine caught with a popping cough. Pres let the Curtiss idle, then opened the throttle to 1400 rpm. She sounded healthy, ready to work for him. He throttled down and taxied across the field into the wind. Curry was already in the air, having utilized the Hisso's power for a full-throttle takeoff. Thompson watched the black-and-gold Standard climb steeply above the trees at the edge of the fairgrounds, then bank back, skimming the branches in a swirl of leaves.

Pres gave the Jenny some juice, and she picked up speed. The earth fell away beneath him, and he began to climb for altitude. Curry had warned him not to try anything near the ground, with no safety margin in case he got into trouble, so he climbed up to a thousand before going into his routine. He would warm up the crowd with some basic stuff, then let Curry take over. Pres had thrown a hasty coat of crimson paint over the olive drab surface of the wings, and he knew they could see him easily down there in the grandstand.

Here, in this vast blue upper ocean, with the wind in his face, Pres Thompson had no thought for patched wings or tired struts or for the makeshift splices in the spars. He felt invincible, high above the earthbound crowd, as they watched him spiral and barrel roll the JN. Now – he would show them what it was to own the sky!

Pres lowered the nose of his plane, waited a few seconds as the wing fabric bulged threateningly between the strained ribs, then pulled the stick back slowly, the throttle wide. His body was mashed deep in the cockpit as the fairgrounds disappeared beyond the trailing edges; then he seemed to hang suspended in space at the top of the loop before the Jenny shuddered down, closing the circle.

Perfect, Pres told himself, just perfect! The old girl still has some spunk left in her, all right.

A thousand feet above the JN, while Stuart Curry steadied the Hisso, Slim Toulmin prepared to go into his act. Toulmin was a small man, standing barely five feet two, with a wind-leathered face, eroded by the elements, the face of a monkey – with wide nostrils and round, bright eyes. His harness securely buckled around his thick waist, he gave the thumbs-up signal to Curry. And the Solitaire wing-waggled to Thompson: we're coming down.

The ships exchanged position as the ballyhoo man megaphoned a lavish introduction, and now the show belonged to Curry and his wing walker. Pres would simply hover in the sky while the act progressed below him. Then, for a finale, after Toulmin had made his parachute jump, the two planes would do a double loop, laying red and blue smoke trails across the fairgrounds before landing again near the main grandstand.

Pres could see Toulmin in position, centered above the cockpit on the top wing of the Standard, anchored by straps and metal heel cups, braced against the wind like a dark ghost as Curry dived on the field. Just before his wheels touched earth, the Solitaire screamed the black-and-gold ship up past the main stands in a high loop, the sharp sound of the Hispano engine ripping a long gash in the stretched blue silk of the sky.

Pres held his breath, circling by instinct, his full attention focused on the machine below him. Now Stuart Curry was using his legendary skill to maximum advantage – tying the control stick into level flying position, hoisting his body over the side of the cockpit into the whipping blast of the slipstream, lowering himself under the belly of the Standard to the landing wheels, hanging there by his knees while he waved down to the crowd. Toulmin above, Curry below – with the plane flying itself. Indeed, *this* was stunting!

The Solitaire climbed back into the cockpit, quickly attached cords to the controls, then inched backward to a sitting position between cockpit and tail, guiding the ship by tugging to right or left on the ropes, riding the Standard as a cowboy rides a bronc.

Pres Thompson watched and wondered: would he ever be this good; would he ever be able to match this demon of the air who employed his personal brand of magic to hurl the heavy Standard across the heavens as easily as a child hurls a stone across a pond?

Then something glinted on the wingtop, pulling Thompson's attention away from Stuart Curry. Slim Toulmin had a whiskey bottle tipped to his lips, and Pres watched in a cold sweat as the swaying stuntman emptied the contents, pitching the bottle into space. It winked like a jewel, falling away into the trees. Curry, in the process of regaining the cockpit, did not see any of this.

That drunken slob can ruin the show, Pres thought angrily, putting the JN into a shallow dive. I'd better warn Curry and have him wave Toulmin in before the main act. A drunk on the wing is worse than a wild prop.

Pres leveled out next to Curry's Standard, and pointed up at Toulmin, making a "bottle" of his hand and raising it to his lips. Curry got the message, but too late. Slim Toulmin had already left his top perch, and was now on the lower right wing, pulling himself from wire to strut, heading for the tip. Curry yelled something, a bitter phrase, which was swept away in the noisy slipstream – and Toulmin paused. Curry gestured violently toward the front cockpit, indicating that Toulmin was to come in, but the stuntman ignored the order, resuming his slow passage.

Curry waved Pres back upstairs, expertly steadying the plane against the outside shift in weight. Thompson could see cold anger etched in the Solitaire's vulpine face, but he knew that Curry could do nothing but hope Toulmin would not foul up. The little man was now beyond reach.

Pres watched Toulmin kneel on the trembling finger of wood and fabric, wave to the grandstand, then reach down to grab the wing skid. Like a fat monkey, he dropped over the edge, to hang by one hand under the ship. A rope ladder had been rolled around the skid, and now Toulmin released it, transferring his grip to the ladder. Now he was swinging from the spider-webbing of rope: hanging by his heels, by one hand, by the other, by both knees, by one knee…commanding the rapt attention of the awed fair-grounds crowd.

Maybe he'll be okay, thought Pres; maybe he's not drunk enough to let it affect his act. He looks fine so far. He *could* be all right.

Toulmin was back on the skid, hauling in the ladder. He pulled himself to the wingtip, stood up, then began to waver uncertainly, a hand to his forehead.

God, he's blacking out, Pres screamed silently. The son of a bitch is blacking out!

Toulmin recovered. Unsteadily, he began to unstrap the parachute which was tied along the surface of the wing, hunching into the shoulder straps, then sitting down on the wingtip, legs dangling

"Jump, you lousy drunk!" Pres shouted, uncaring that the words were lost the moment they left his lips. "Get off that wing!"

Slim Toulmin raised his arm for a final wave – then thrust himself into space. But the alcohol had done its work; the jump was never completed. Toulmin had jerked his chute cord too quickly, and the lines had snagged along the wing, slamming the stuntman's head hard against the fuselage. Toulmin swung twisting like a rag doll below the right wingtip, unconscious, his lines snarled by the wind.

Pres felt completely frustrated; there wasn't a thing he could do. If the Jenny's top wing had been reinforced to bear the extra weight he might try to bring the JN up under the swinging body and… No, even that wouldn't work, because he'd need someone up there on top to cut the tangled chute lines.

Curry was equally helpless. He couldn't leave the cockpit to haul Toulmin in, and he couldn't land without killing them both. But the Standard would not be able to stay up much longer since the light fuel load was almost exhausted.

He'll think of something, Pres desperately told himself. The Solitaire will think of some way out...

Stuart Curry cautiously lowered the Standard's left wing, holding the ship at a severe angle, with the right wing high – and Toulmin's body swung slowly in toward the cockpit. His face twisted with effort, Curry freed one hand from the controls and reached out to grasp Slim Toulmin's jacket. Pres could see what Curry was trying to do, and it seemed impossible. He would have to hold the ship's left wing hard down, gripping the control stick with his knees, and attempt to cut the chute lines with one hand, hanging on to Toulmin with the other. Impossible!

No, not impossible – because Curry was *doing* it, slashing at the thick twist of tangled line with an open pocket knife as he held Slim Toulmin tight against the cockpit.

But an airman's luck is bound to run out...

The Standard's overstrained right wing suddenly split wide along the fuselage with a terrible rending sound, and the plane went into a vicious spin as the wing disintegrated, splintering, crumpling like black tissue paper back into the golden body.

The plane continued to fall earthward.

Pres Thompson saw the end of it, saw the crash that the man they called the Solitaire had long dreaded, saw the proud black-and-gold bird explode and burn.

By the time he had landed – diving the Jenny down until the wires sang, bumping roughly across the field to the crash area – it was already as Curry had told him it would be. They were there in the smoke, men, women, children – tearing and clawing at the scattered pieces of wing and fuselage. When Pres fought his way to the body of Stuart Nelson Curry it was stripped clean. The goggles and white scarf, the gold helmet, the neat gray cavalry breeches, the polished leather boots – all gone.

Curry had been thrown clear. His neck was twisted at an odd, unnatural angle, but his face was unmarked: eyes wide and staring, nostrils dilated, mouth agape in a frozen scream.

"He knew," moaned Thompson, turning away as the sirens increased their slow wail. "My God, he *knew*!"

The Dorado County Fair was over, the tents down, the grandstands left to sun and dust, the booths closed and boarded. Pres stood by the Jenny, adjusting his helmet.

"Want a hand with the prop?" someone asked him. Pres did not look up at he nodded.

"Thanks," he said, his tone flat and emotionless.

He was thinking about a new DeHaviland cadet trainer with 400 powerful horses under the throttle. And he was also thinking about the girl who loved him back in Georgia, who had begged him not to become a stunter. He'd write to her, tell her she didn't need to worry. He'd write very soon.

Pres looked up at the waiting sky, serene and stippled with white clouds – and then he climbed aboard the Jenny, pulling down his goggles.

As the Curtiss engine coughed raggedly to life he thought about a future which, suddenly, seemed to have meaning and purpose.

And, finally, he thought about the man they had called the Solitaire.

I BELIEVE IN REINCARNATION – that we have all lived past lives. A few years ago, when I was regressed by author and university professor Kathleen Jenks (a reincarnation expert), I found that in the late 1800s I had lived what turned out to be a rather dull life as the sheriff of an insignificant Wild West town. Which may, or may not, explain my abiding love for the genre.

I've seen every Western movie ever made, many of them several times (particularly the great films of John Ford). I've ridden with *The Wild Bunch*, gunned down Jack Palance in *Shane*, escaped from the law with *Butch Cassidy and the Sundance Kid*, and sweated out the arrival of the killers by train in *High Noon*. I vividly recall, at the age of seven, tottering down the aisle at my local film palace to watch Tom Mix in *The Miracle Rider*. To me, Mix and Buck Jones were boyhood idols – and I had my own Western outfit: chaps, sombrero, and toy six-guns.

"Shadow Quest" owes a huge debt to Max Brand (whose Western fiction I've been devouring since the age of fourteen). Brand's wild stallions find their echo in my wild stallion, Diablo.

Here is more than just another short story.

It is, clearly, a labor of love.

SHADOW QUEST

HIS NAME WAS STRIKING: John Shadow. Otherwise, he was a very ordinary fellow. No wife. No family. A drifter, making his way through life as best he could. No goals. No ambitions. He gambled some, losing more than he won. He boxed for pocket money in Dodge City, cut timber in Canada, punched cows along the Cimarron, rode the rods west as a road tramp, served as a bouncer in Santa Fe, and played piano at a fancy house in El Paso. That job ended abruptly when Shadow ran off with one of the house ladies (her name was Margie). But they didn't stay together. Margie left him for a buffalo hunter two weeks later.

He was at loose ends. He owned the clothes on his back, a lump-headed mustang, and a new Winchester he'd won in a Kansas poker game. And not much else.

That was when John Shadow decided to ride into the Sierra Madres after Diablo.

He heard about him in the border town of Los Lobos along the American side of the Rio Grande. A wild stallion. El Diablo Blanco – the White Devil. Fast, smart…and mean.

Two trappers at the bar were talking about the stallion.

"Has he been hunted?" Shadow asked.

"By the best," said the bartender, a beefy man in a stained apron. "With relays of horses. Sometimes they've run him a hundred miles in one day, but he always out-smarts 'em. Disappears like smoke in the wind. Lemme tellya, if a horse can laugh, he's laughing."

"I'm good with horses," Shadow said quietly.

The barman's smile was cynical. "Got a real way with 'em, eh?"

"I'd say so," nodded Shadow.

"Well, then, here's your chance." And he exchanged grins with the two trappers. "Just take yourself a little jaunt up into the Sierras an' fetch out the white."

"I need to think on it," Shadow told him.

He returned to the bar later that same afternoon. "I'm going after him," he said.

It was a full day's ride into the upper foothills of the Sierra Madres. Shadow was following a crude, hand-drawn map provided by the barman after he'd convinced him he was serious in his quest for the white. The barman had indicated the area where the horse had been most often seen – but Shadow had no guarantee that Diablo had remained in this section of the mountains.

He was well aware of the various methods used in the

capture of wild horses. Often, a sizable group of riders pursued the target animals, attempting to force them into a circular run, gradually tightening the circle. Sometimes hunters used relays of horses, constantly maintaining fresh mounts in the hope of running down the winded herd.

There was the story of a legendary hunt by a young Cheyenne warrior in which the Indian had traveled on foot for many hundreds of miles over a period of several months in pursuit of a single horse. The natural speed of a wild horse is reduced by its need to graze each day. Whenever the animal stopped to eat, the Indian's tireless, loping stride would close the distance between them. The Cheyenne lived on water and parched corn, eating as he ran, thus constantly forcing the pursuit.

Eventually, so the story went, both hunter and hunted became gaunt and weakened. The long trail ended on the naked slope of a snowcapped peak high above timberline when the Indian managed to lasso his totally exhausted quarry.

Of course, even if this fanciful tale were true, Shadow had no patience for such an arduous pursuit.

When he was within range of the horse, Shadow intended to bring down the animal with a bullet from his Winchester. The shot would require extreme accuracy, since his bullet must crease the nape of the neck at a spot that would jar the animal's spinal column. This would stun the horse, allowing its capture.

Diablo was unusual in that he ran alone. Most wild horses run with others of their kind, in herds numbering up to fifty or more, but the white stallion had always been a loner, staying well clear of the herds ranging the Sierra Madres. He wanted no young colts or laboring mares to slow his swift progress.

Many attempts had been made to capture him. One group of hunters, led by Colonel Matthew Sutton, had plans for Diablo as an Eastern show horse, and ran the stallion for six weeks without letup. Eleven horses had galloped themselves to death during that brutal pursuit, while the proud white drifted ahead of them, beyond their reach, defiant and strong.

One frustrated hunter claimed that the stallion had never truly existed – that he was nothing more than an apparition, a white ghost who galloped like a cloud across the sky.

When John Shadow repeated this last claim to a trapper he'd met in the high mountains, a one-armed veteran named Hatcher, the old man declared: "Oh, he's real enough all right, Diablo is. I've seen him by sun and by moon, in good weather and bad. There was one time I come up on him close enough to near touch that smooth silk hide of his, but then he took off like a streak of white lightning."

The old man cackled at the memory. "A pure wonder, he is. Ain't no horse like him nowhere in these mountains or out of 'em, and that's a fact."

"Then you don't think I can catch him?" asked John Shadow.

"Sure ya can – as easy as you can reach out and catch the wind." And Hatcher cackled again.

There was a great difference between the arid, sterile

mountains around El Paso and this lush terrain of the Sierra
Madres. Here Shadow found water in abundance, and rich
grass, and thickly wooded hills – a veritable paradise that
provided Diablo with everything he needed to sustain his
wild existence.

Despite the old trapper's firm conviction that the great
horse could never be captured, Hatcher had nonetheless provided solid hope. The trapper had agreed that Diablo did
indeed frequent this particular section of mountain wilderness.

Luck and a keen eye might well reward him here. Just a
day later, as he was riding out of a shallow draw onto the
level of a grassed plateau, John Shadow had his first look at
the legendary stallion.

Diablo had been nibbling the green, tender sprouts that
tipped a thick stand of juniper and now he raised his head
to scent the wind. He nickered softly. Nostrils flaring, he
suddenly wheeled about to face the rider at the far end of
the plateau.

Shadow had slipped the new Winchester from its scab-
bard, since the range permitted him to fire, but he slowly
lowered the weapon, awed by the animal's size and beauty.
Easily seventeen hands tall, deep-chested, sheathed with
rippling muscle, and as white as a drift of newly fallen snow,
Diablo was truly magnificent.

The horse stood immobile for a long moment, studying
his enemy. Then, with a toss of his thick mane and a ringing neigh of defiance, he trotted away, breaking into a
smooth-flowing gallop that carried him swiftly out of sight.

Dammit! I could have fired, Shadow told himself; I

could have ended it here and now with a single shot.

The light had been ideal and he was certain he could have creased the animal's neck. And there had been ample time for the shot. But the sheer power and majesty of the horse had kept him from firing. What if his bullet had missed its mark and struck a vital area? What if he had killed this king of stallions? Many wild horses have been fatally shot by hunters attempting to stun them.

No, he decided, I need to be closer, a lot closer, to make absolutely *certain* of the shot. And now that he's aware of me, it's not going to be easy.

That night, after a meal of mountain grouse roasted over his campfire, Shadow spread his blanket across a bed of fragrant pine needles on the forest floor. Lying on his back, hands laced behind his head, under a mass of tall pines that crowded the stars, he considered the meaning of freedom.

He had always thought of himself as a free man, yet through much of his life he'd been bound by the commands of others – when he had served in the war, when he was working in bars and brothels, when he'd been a cowpuncher and lumberman. In Diablo, John Shadow had witnessed true freedom. The great horse owed allegiance to no one. The whole wide world of the mountain wilderness served as his personal playground. He ran at no man's bidding, served no master but himself.

And now I'm trying to take that freedom away from him, thought Shadow. I'm trying to saddle and bridle him, bend his will to mine, feed him oats instead of his wild sweet grass, make him gallop at my command.

Did he have the right? Did *anyone* really have the right to own such a glorious animal?

With these melancholy thoughts drifting through his consciousness, Shadow closed his eyes, breathing deeply of the clean mountain air. The faint whisper of wind, rustling the trees, lulled him to sleep.

He awakened abruptly, shocked and wide-eyed, to an earth-shaking roar.

The morning sun was slanting down in dusty yellow bars through the pine branches, painting the forest floor in shades of brilliant orange. At the edge of the clearing, not twenty-five feet from where John Shadow had been sleeping, a huge, brown-black grizzly had reared up to a full-battle position, its clawed forepaws extended like a boxer's hands. The monstrous jaws gaped wide in anger, yellow fangs gleaming like swords in the wide red cave of its mouth.

The mighty bruin, a full thousand pounds of bone and muscle, was not facing directly toward Shadow, but was angled away from him, in the direction of another enemy. Diablo!

Incredible as it seemed, the tall white stallion was trotting around the grizzly in a wary half-circle, ears flattened, eyes glaring, prehensile upper lip pulled back from its exposed teeth.

The horse was plainly preparing to attack.

Shadow was amazed. He had never known a horse to challenge a grizzly. Even the scent of an approaching bear was enough to send the fiercest stallion into a gallop for safety – yet here was Diablo, boldly facing this forest mammoth with no trace of fear.

Then an even greater shock struck the hunter: Diablo was defending *him*! The bear had apparently been making his forest rounds, overturning rocks for insects, ripping apart dead logs for grubs and worms, when he'd encountered the sleeping figure of John Shadow. He was about to descend on the hunter when the stallion intervened.

It made no logical sense. Yet, somehow, the white horse had felt protective of the man who had been hunting him. That Diablo had come to his rescue was a fact John Shadow accepted, although he was truly stunned by such an act. The scene seemed to be part of a dream, yet Shadow knew he was fully awake. What was happening, *was* happening.

Now Diablo reared up, with a ringing neigh, to strike at the brute's head with his stone-sharpened forehooves. A hoof connected with the bruin's skull like a dropped hammer, and the bear staggered back, roaring horribly, its eyes like glowing sparks of fire.

Then the grizzly counterattacked, lunging ponderously forward to rake one of its great paws across the stallion's neck. This blow, powerful enough to take a man's head off at the shoulders, buckled Diablo's legs, and the stunned animal toppled backward and down, blood running from an open neck wound.

The bear lumbered forward to finish his opponent, but by now Shadow had his Winchester in hand, and he began firing at the dark-shagged beast.

The giant grizzly seemed impervious to bullets. With a frightful bellow of rage, he charged wildly at the hated man-thing.

Shadow stopped firing to roll sideways – barely avoiding the razored claws, which scored the log next to his head. With the huge bruin looming above him like a brown-black mountain, Shadow pumped three more rounds into the beast at heart level.

They did the job.

Like a chopped tree, the monster crashed to the forest floor, expiring with a final, defiant death-growl. It had taken five rifle bullets to kill him.

Diablo lay on his side, only half conscious, breathing heavily, as Shadow tended the stallion's injured shoulder. Using fresh water from his canteen, he cleansed the wound, then treated it with an old Indian remedy: he carefully packed a mix of forest herbs and mud over the wound, and tied it in place with a shirt from his saddle roll.

Amazingly, the animal did not resist these efforts. Diablo seemed to understand that Shadow was trying to help him.

If those claws had gone a half-inch deeper, Shadow knew, the shoulder muscle would have been ruined, crippling the great horse.

He ran his hand soothingly along the stallion's quivering flank, murmuring in a soft voice, "Easy, boy, easy now. You're going to be all right…you're going to be fine…"

And Diablo rolled an anxious eye toward John Shadow.

It took more than a week before the white stallion was willing to follow a lead rope. During this entire period Shadow worked night and day to win the gallant animal's trust, talking, stroking, picking lush seed grass for the horse to eat. The shoulder wound healed rapidly.

On the ninth day after the bear attack, Shadow began his ride back to Los Lobos, with Diablo trotting behind him on the lead rope.

Shadow was smiling as he rode. Now, suddenly, his life held purpose and meaning. Soon he would teach Diablo to accept him as a rider; he would be the first to guide this glorious beast over valley and plain – and riding him, Shadow knew, would be like riding the wind itself. There would be a mutual trust between them. A deep understanding. A bonding of spirits.

Before he had made this trip into the Sierra Madres, John Shadow had never believed in miracles.

Now, looking back at the splendor of Diablo, he knew he had been wrong.

I WAS A DEDICATED TV FAN of *The A-Team*, with its stylized violence (no blood or death), peppery dialogue, and far-out characters. In fact, "Helle on Wheels" began as an *A-Team* teleplay. I wrote the script strictly for the pleasure it gave me, with no real expectation of its being produced – and it wasn't.

Time passed. Then it suddenly struck me that this "lost" teleplay would make a spirited Nick Challis adventure. (Nick, my detective protagonist, is the younger brother of an earlier private eye of mine, Bart Challis – who was featured in *Playboy* and in two of my crime novels.) Thus, my *A-Team* script evolved into a Nick Challis detective tale.

I have chosen "Helle on Wheels" as the final selection in *Ships in the Night* in order to end the collection on a lighter note.

Just for the Helle of it.

HELLE ON WHEELS

ONE OF THE FIRST THINGS Judy Helle told me about was her "e."

"It's silent," she said. "Pronounced as in 'go to'."

"Hell of a name," I said.

"Exactly." She nodded.

But that came later. What I want you to hear now is the early part in her words not mine, because I wasn't there when it happened. This was tape-recorded in my office, so it's just the way Judy told it to me.

We have this kinda small-time stunt show in South Carolina [said Judy]. Me and my sisters, Lyn and Liza. Call ourselves the Helledrivers. We run it with our Uncle Jack. He was Dad's brother and Daddy is dead. So's Mom. Anyway, Uncle Jack's a real good mechanic and takes care of the cars for us while we do the driving. We used to have a crew, to set up the ramps and stuff, but they left when Ben Stark began threatening us. Stark's bigtime. Runs a whole string of major stunt shows in the South. He tried to buy us out, but we said no, even though the money was good. The show's all we got and we love doing it. When we refused to sell Stark made a lot of threats…

Anyhow, on the morning I want to tell about, a Saturday, we were getting ready for our noon show. It was still early and there was just the four of us on the field below the empty grandstands, setting up the jump ramps and fire hoops and all that. Suddenly, Uncle Jack runs over to me where I was at the fence and says, "We got trouble. Three trucks – headin' this way fast."

"Stark's men?" I wanted to know.

"Looks like his trucks."

The three wide-bed rigs slam full-tilt through the locked gate, knocking it haywire, and skid to a stop in front of the four of us. Lyn and Liza look kinda shaky. The guys in the trucks – about a dozen of 'em – get out carrying axes and sledgehammers.

A big beefcake named Salter was the boss. I'd seen him before with Ben Stark. One of his chief muscle boys.

Salter walks over from the trucks with another oversize ape named Grady, who was hefting a long-handle sledge. Salter had an axe.

"Afraid we got some bad news for you folks," Salter says.

"And just what would that be?" asks Uncle Jack.

"Your show's been canceled. Due to faulty equipment."

"Yeah," pipes in Grady. "As concerned citizens, we got

public safety to think about."

Uncle Jack had his dander up. "There's nothing wrong with this show's equipment and you know it," he says, glaring at them.

"Well now, that's a matter of opinion," says Grady – and he walks over to one of our stunt cars. "You take a worn out vehicle like this. Plain unsafe to operate." And he swings his sledge against the front windshield, splintering the glass. "See! You got unsafe vision here. Might run right into somebody."

Then Salter sinks the blade of his axe into the right front tire, slashing the rubber. "Plus you got a real bad traction problem."

Uncle Jack is all red in the face mad, and me an' my sisters are plenty steamed too. When Grady starts to swing the sledge again Uncle Jack grabs his arm to stop him and Salter comes up from behind and hits him across the head with the axe handle.

I jump at them, and so do Lyn and Liza, but they just shove us aside and go to work on our cars and equipment, smashing everything up real bad.

When it's over, just before they climb back in their trucks, Salter comes up to me and my sisters. We're trying to help Uncle Jack, trying to stop his head from bleeding, and Salter is grinning at us.

"When Mr. Stark calls you again to make his next offer I'd advise you to take it serious. *Real serious.*"

And they all drive off.

This is where I take up the story.

Judy came to Los Angeles to hire me, and the day she arrived I was at the observatory in Griffith Park. Business was zilch so I'd left Mike Cahill at the office and headed for the planetarium to take in the laser star show. Mike had recommended it. Super spectacular, he said it was.

I had some time to kill before the thing started and I was poking around in the Globe Room – where they have this big model of the Earth suspended from the ceiling – when Judy walked up to me.

"You're Nick Challis, aren't you?" she asked. Big smile. Great figure. Blonde. Maybe twenty-five or younger. I said I was Nick.

"You look exactly like your photo," she told me.

"What photo?"

"The one your Indian cousin sent to my Uncle Jack. He knows this cousin of yours, from New Mexico. Tom Walking Stick. Mr. Stick told us where to reach you and sent us your photo. So I came here to hire you."

"From where?"

"From Forrest City, South Carolina. It's not far from Darlington where they have the stock car races."

I nodded. "My brother Bart, he follows the stockers. Got a poster from Darlington on his office wall. Signed by Dick Petty."

"Uncle Jack says we can trust you because you've got some Apache in your bloodline. Uncle Jack is one-quarter Apache. Your partner, Mr. Michael Cahill – when I called your office – he told me where I could find you."

"You sure talk a lot."

She smiled. "I always have. As a kid, Mom could never shut me up. Well?"

"Well, what?"

"Will you work for us? For me and my two sisters and Uncle Jack?"

"Doing what?"

"Combating injustice. Righting wrongs."

"I'm a private detective, not the Lone Ranger. And I don't even know what your problem is."

"That's a long story – and I think your Mr. Cahill should hear it too."

Which is when I took her back to the office in Studio City, snapped on the tape recorder, and told Judy to start talking. It was like asking a race horse to gallop. She proceeded to tell us all about Ben Stark and his goon squad.

After she'd finished Mike asked her: "What about the law?"

An ex-cop from St. Louis, Missouri, Cahill had joined my lone wolf agency just a month ago. He had some savings to invest in a business and I had a business that needed saving. It was a marriage made in heaven. He was a little spooky around the edges, with an explosive Irish temper, but he was basically a nice guy. So we were giving it a whirl as Challis and Cahill. And now he was asking Judy about the law…

"It's a joke," she told us. "Stark owns the law in Forrest County. When Ben Stark sneezes, halfway across the state the Sheriff says 'Gesundheit!'"

I gave her a steady look. "Just what is it, specifically, you want us to do for you?"

"Come back home with me. Guard us from Stark's men.

And try and find out what's behind his offer to buy us out. Is that specific enough?"

"Why does there have to be something behind his offer?" asked Cahill.

"Stark doesn't need our show. We barely make expenses. We're no competition to him. I *know* he has an ulterior motive. You're detectives. You can find out what it is."

Cahill leaned back in our new swivel chair (the old one didn't swivel) and nodded sagely. He had moody cow eyes, a tiny, carefully-combed brush mustache, and no hair from the ears up. He could look very sage.

"It's awfully muggy this time of year in South Carolina," he said. "But, cosmically, I feel we should help these people. I'm getting good vibes."

"Cahill is into cosmic vibrations," I told Judy. "Considers himself a kind of universal geiger counter."

"That's my reading," he nodded. "What do you say, Nick?"

Judy stared at me. "Yes, what do you say?"

"I say let's go to South Carolina."

Cahill was right about the weather; it was muggy. And hot. My shirt collar had melted into my neck by the time we crossed the Forrest County line in Judy's battered Ford station wagon.

"Welcome to the home of the Helledrivers," she said as we rolled through the gate into the main fairgrounds. A rusted metal sign next to the grandstands announced:

THRILLS! SPILLS! CHILLS!

SEE THE DEVIL'S TRIO – THE WORLD FAMOUS
HELLEDRIVERS
DEFY DEATH ITSELF
EVERY SATURDAY AND SUNDAY
IN THE BIGGEST LITTLE THRILL SHOW
IN THE SOUTH!

"We're not actually world famous," admitted Judy. "In fact, we're not even known in other parts of the South. That's 'cuz we don't travel like some shows. We're home folks, really."

I could see why she was confused about Stark's wanting to buy them out. What was to buy? A patch of dusty fairgrounds, some weathered grandstands, four dented stunt cars, a small equipment shack, a garage with a sagging roof and a paint-blistered house trailer with a shabby looking service truck parked behind it.

"I have this ugly habit of wanting to get paid for my work," I said, as we stopped near the trailer. "I don't see much evidence of wealth around here."

She set the brake and we got out. "Uncle Jack got a bank loan to fix up our cars and equipment after Stark's gorillas smashed everything up," she said. "We've got enough left over to pay your fees."

"That's reassuring," said Cahill. Sweat glistened on his ruddy Irish face, and his mustache looked wilted.

Inside the trailer we met Uncle Jack, Lyn and Liza. He was somewhere in his fifties with a deep tan and big freckled hands. His handshake was rock-solid, and his eyes were direct and honest. The sisters were young, pert, and pretty. Lyn had red hair (dyed?) and Liza was blonde, like Judy. They were both on the tall side, with great figures. I sensed they were a lot tougher than they looked. Had to be – to survive in their game.

Over drinks (mellow Southern corn whiskey, no soda), we talked about Ben Stark.

"Way I see it, he *owes* you for what his boys did," I told them.

Cahill nodded sagely.

"No lawyer has ever collected a penny from Stark," Uncle Jack declared.

I grinned. "Who said anything about a lawyer?"

Stark's home base in Darlington was suitably impressive. A sprawling complex of fat steel-and-glass buildings dominated by a tall black tower like an upraised coffin. It was topped by a huge golden S and a huge golden E. For Stark Enterprises. Reminded me of a glitzy hotel on the Vegas strip.

We informed the lizard-eyed gate guard that we had an appointment with Mr. Stark. Which was true. Amazing how fast you can get in to see busy people once you tell them you're with the IRS.

The guard waved us inside. We were in Judy's Ford wagon, me and Mike, with Cahill driving. We parked behind the main tower and got out, each of us with a briefcase.

"There it is," I said.

"Yeah," said Cahill, running a tiny comb through his

brush mustache. "And it's a beaut."

We were talking about Ben Stark's custom speedboat, a racy-looking, chrome-and-wood job on a trailer parked next to the tower. A husky wide-shouldered guard stood beside it. The boat was Stark's personal pride and joy. Judy told us he kept it parked there during the week because he liked being able to look down from his office window and admire it.

"I'm going in," I told Mike. "You know what to do."

"Right," he nodded.

I gave my phony IRS name (Ed Gains) to the receptionist, got a building pass, and was told to go right up to Suite 500. Mr. Stark was waiting to see me.

A Bach concerto was piped into the private elevator taking me to the fifth floor. Classy, but I would have preferred early Elvis.

An equally-classy secretary in Suite 500 buzzed me into Stark's private office. He got up from a leather-topped desk large enough to bowl on and walked around it to pump my hand. (Always be nice to the IRS.) He was football big. Six three, maybe 280, with frosted gray hair and a wide chin. His smile was as phony as the name I gave him. I got the impression he didn't smile often.

"Afraid I'm not going to be much help to you, Mr. Gains," he told me. "My accounting firm handles our taxes, and they have all the data."

"That's okay," I said. "I didn't come for data, I came for money."

"Money?" He looked startled. "I don't understand."

"I'll make it quick and simple. I'm not with the IRS. I'm a personal representative of the Helle sisters. You owe them for damage to their cars and equipment and I'm here to collect. I'll take ten grand. In cash. Can you understand that?"

He pressed a button on his desk and his two chief goons walked into the office. I didn't require intros. From Judy's description, I pegged them as Salter and Grady. They looked hungry, and I was their steak and potatoes.

"Show the gentleman out," said Stark. His tone was as cold as his eyes. "And make sure he gets a few bruises on the way."

"Call 'em off, Stark," I said, reaching into my briefcase.

"Give me a reason," he said.

I removed a small black object the size of a cigarette package. "Go to the window," I said. "Look down and tell me what you see."

Stark was curious, so he did that. "My boat's down there."

I joined him at the window. "But your guard is missing, isn't he?"

Stark glared down into the parking lot five stories below. Mike Cahill waved up at him.

"That fancy water wagon is worth a lot more than ten grand," I said. "Either I walk out of here with the cash now, or you lose your pride and joy. It's wired to blow. My man down there took care of it. Cash or the boat. Your choice."

And I held my finger over a small red button on the black object. I waved down to Mike and he moved quickly away from the boat.

"Nobody threatens Ben Stark," he said softly. "Nobody."

I grinned. "That's right out of a 1930s Cagney movie," I said. "You self-styled tough guys give me a tickle in the gut."

He glared at me. "You're bluffing," he said. Then, to his goons: "Take him!"

As Salter and Grady came for me across a rug thick enough to hide prairie dogs in I ducked behind Stark's desk and thumbed the red button. Five stories below, with a roar, Stark's speedboat erupted into a multitude of jigsaw pieces. He saw it go, and screamed like I'd knifed him.

Grady and Salter were stopped cold by the explosion which had rocked the building. They looked stunned.

"You're dead meat," Stark whispered. His eyes were wild and glittering.

"Keep those two walking balls of horse vomit away from me," I warned Stark, my finger poised near another button on the detonator. "I figure we're even for this round, so I'm leaving. Safely. If you try to stop me the *building* goes. The main supports are wired. I press this button and your tower takes a tumble."

"The asshole's putting us on," snarled Grady. He started for me. "I'll break his goddamn neck!"

"No!" Stark's voice stopped him again, his face white and pinched. "We can't take the chance. Let him go."

I edged toward Salter who was blocking the door. "You heard him, scumhead," I snapped. "Clear back!" Stark nodded, and Salter stepped reluctantly aside as I opened the door. "Now, I'm going down to my partner and we're driving out of here. If anyone tries to stop us I blow the building." I held up the detonator. "This baby has a five-mile range. Understood?"

Stark's lips were a tight blue line against the paleness of his face; he was literally trembling with rage.

"Mister," he told me, "you're going to have a real short life."

"Just keep your punks away from the Helle sisters or you'll lose more than a frigging boat. Mess with me and I'll take your head off at the ankles."

And I left his office chuckling over my exit line.

A few miles out from Stark's we spotted the truck behind us. No surprise. It figured that he'd send some of his muscle after us once we cleared the area. The stuff about blowing up his headquarters *had* been a bluff, but that didn't matter now. The truck was closing fast on us. Modified Jeepster, souped-up for speed. Our Ford wagon was way outclassed.

"What are we gonna do?" Cahill asked me. "They're shooting at us, Nick."

He didn't have to tell me. Bullets were spatting into the back of the station wagon. "We shoot back," I said, and leaned out of the passenger window to squeeze off three rounds from my .38 short-barrel.

"That won't get the job done," Mike declared. "We need a 12-gauge pump."

"Sure, and maybe Santa will bring us one for Christmas, but in the meantime we're screwed. They're right on our ass!"

That's when I spotted the overpass – a long finger of raw white concrete arching over the highway.

"Take the next right," I told Mike. "We can lose 'em at

that overpass."

"You kidding?" growled Mike. "Damn thing's got a hole in the middle."

Mike was right; the construction wasn't complete. There was a sizable gap between the two ends – with just air between.

"You can jump it," I said.

"I'm not Evel Knievel," he growled. "And this is no rocket car."

"Just keep your foot down," I said.

We crashed through the wooden road barrier leading up to the overpass, then headed straight for the concrete edge.

"Holy shit!" yelled Mike, as we sailed off into thin blue air. "We're not gonna make it!"

But we did. The station wagon landed on the far side of the overpass with a terrific thump that jarred my back teeth. But we were upright and rolling free.

I looked back. The goon driving Stark's truck wasn't as crazy as we were and he skidded his rig to a tire-grinding stop at the lip of the overpass.

So we got away clean.

But we knew we'd be seeing a lot more of Ben Stark and Company.

There aren't many of them around any more – the old-style gyms smelling of sweat and sour canvas, catering to hungry, hard-muscled youngsters with a yen to enter the fight game. But Forrest City had one and the guy who owned it was a punchy ex-bantamweight named Benny "Boom-Boom"

Fenster. With the face of a battered frog.

A few kids with big shoulders and small brains were pounding the bags and jumping rope as I talked to Boom-Boom, while two guys were grunting and body-punching each other in a center ring.

"What you want my two best boys fer?" Benny asked me. Cahill was standing near the far wall in Fenster's shabby office, looking over some dusty fight photos.

"We expect a little trouble at the Helledrivers show this weekend," I told him. "Two of your beefcakes will help even the odds."

"They gonna do some fightin', huh?"

"You got it." I opened my wallet. "Well?"

Benny nodded. "Oke, pal. You pay me. I take out my cut an' I pay them."

We worked out a sum and I handed over the cash. "Have 'em there by ten on Saturday," I said.

"Oke," said Boom-Boom.

"Great," I said, and waved to Mike.

And we left.

Benny kept his promise. Two of his best muscle boys arrived right on time Saturday morning. Tall and wide. Built like Mack trucks. One was named Santos; the other called himself the Philly Kid, but admitted he'd never been to Philly.

I told them to sit in the main stands near the exit stairs during the show and to watch for my signal in case of trouble.

Stark was pissed. I figured he'd send back his goons for a prime bust-up – to get even for what we'd done to his cute little waterbug. Which was okay with me. I was getting stale; a nice physical workout would tone up my system. I was actually looking forward to what promised to be a stimulating afternoon.

Outside of television, I'd never seen an auto thrill show, and I was impressed. Cahill and I had front-row seats in the stands. We were having a good time, munching hot dogs and watching the three red-white-and-blue cars leap through flaming hoops, sail over stacked barrels and smash through brick walls. The crowd shouted and stomped at each new stunt and the excitement was catching.

Then the voice of the booth announcer (Uncle Jack) boomed over the loudspeakers: "And now, ladies and gentlemen, our final event of the afternoon…as our daring trio of fearless young beauties – Hell's Helledrivers – thrill you and chill you with their spectacular…deadly…death-defying…Rolling Flyover!"

I glanced behind me, up into the stands, spotting Santos and the Philly Kid, enjoying the show as much as we were, sipping Dr. Pepper and jamming popcorn into their mouths.

So far at least, there was no sign of Stark's goon squad. All three stunt vehicles were now lined up on the field below us, with Lyn, Liza and Judy standing next to the cars, dressed in sexy, body-hugging red leather outfits. They gave the crowd a confident thumbs-up, tightened their helmets, then climbed back into their shiny speedwagons for the afternoon's main stunt.

The Rolling Flyover lived up to its hype – a real crowd-pleaser. The red car, driven by Liza, roared up a high jump ramp and flew into the air above Lyn and Judy's white and blue cars as they throttled directly toward one another. At the last split-second, just before a head-on crash seemed inevitable, each barely missed the other by running their outside wheels up a set of raised ground ramps. They flipped into a rollover, then to a final stop, side by side.

Liza's red car, after having sailed right over them in the air during their head-on run, braked to a stop at the bottom of the opposite jump ramp. Then all three Helledrivers slid out of their cars to salute the cheering crowd.

Cahill nudged me as I was applauding. "I think we're due for a cosmic disturbance."

I could see what he meant. Beyond the fairgrounds, three of Stark's trucks were homing in on the area, moving fast. As they neared the gate I stood up and raised an arm to Santos and the Kid. They nodded and broke for the exit stairs.

By the time Stark's men had pulled to a stop in front of the main stands we were all out of sight behind one of the big wooden field ramps, me, Cahill, and Boom-Boom's two muscle boys.

"Don't sock anybody until I do," I told them.

"Yo," said the Philly Kid, cracking his knuckles. His eyes were gleaming. Santos licked his lips like a hungry cat.

Stark obviously didn't worry about breaking the law in Forrest County; he'd sent his wrecking crew to the fairgrounds to do their dirty work in front of a packed grand-stand. The crowd took in the whole act, as if it were part of the show.

Salter got out of the truck with Grady right behind him. They walked over to the three Helle sisters. They both carried axes.

"Guess you ladies don't learn so good," Salter declared. "About the advantages of sellin' out to Mr. Stark."

"Or about the *dis*advantages of *not* sellin' out," added Grady. He was grinning like a baboon.

Judy answered for her sisters, her jaw thrust forward in stubborn anger. "We don't intend to sell. Now or ever. But if we did, it wouldn't be to a prime creep like Ben Stark. You read me?"

Salter chuckled, slowly turning the axe in his big hands. "After we're done here today you'll sell all right. And you'll be glad to get whatever Mr. Stark is kind enough to offer."

"Yeah," added Grady. "You bimbos are about to *retire* from showbiz."

Six other tough-looking mugs from the trucks had gathered behind the two leaders – all with axes and sledgehammers. Salter raised a hand and they started moving toward the stunt cars.

Which is when we stepped out from the ramp. Four of us to their eight. But the odds didn't bother me.

"You airbrains seem to have a real problem in understanding the word 'no'," I said to Salter.

He was smiling. "I was hoping to see you again, mister. Be a real pleasure, bustin' *you* up along with the cars."

And he swung the axe at my skull. I stepped under the swing and snapped his head back with a punch I felt all the way to my shoulder. He dropped the axe, staggering back. I followed with a belly punch, and when he doubled over, I kicked him hard.

In the groin.

The Philly Kid decked Grady with a rapid combination of blows that put him down and out, while Santos tossed a goon over his head into a pile of stunt barrels. Cahill slammed another of Stark's boys over a car's hood, while I tossed a third headfirst through a breakaway brick wall. Santos swung back to drop two others into the dust with triphammer head blows, while the Kid tackled the last of the creeps, putting out his lights.

And that's how it went.

We picked up the scumbags, one by one, and tossed them into their trucks. When they drove out of the fairgrounds they were still in shock.

That was when I became aware of the cheering in the stands. The crowd was going bats over us. We got a standing ovation. They figured it for a rip-roaring climax to the day's action.

Dutifully, we took our bows, and hugs from all three of the Helle sisters, as Uncle Jack's voice boomed from the speakers: "And that concludes our show for the afternoon, ladies and gentlemen. Come back and see us again. And have a *real* nice day!"

That evening after dinner, with the two muscle boys paid off and gone, Cahill and I sat over wine with the Helle sisters in their mobile home. Some talking needed to be done, questions answered, plans made. First, I wanted to know more about Judy and the others.

"How come you three got into this business?" I asked.

"Daddy and his brother, our Uncle Jack, used to barnstorm the South as stunt drivers," Judy told us. "Mom died when we were little, so they took us on the road with them. Taught us everything about stunting."

"That's right," added Liza. "Finally Daddy and Uncle Jack saved enough to buy this land and put together their own show. Then Uncle Jack's eyes went bad – not blind or anything, but just bad enough to keep him from stunting…"

"Daddy had a heart attack after that," said Lyn, "and we ended up with his half, along with Uncle Jack owning the other half. So that's how it is."

"No marriages?" asked Cahill.

"I was married," Lyn said. "For a year. To a real schmuck named Freddie. I dumped him after he lost all our money on the horses. That was in Lexington, Kentucky. I came back here to the show, dead broke."

"We were glad to get her back," Liza said.

"Me and Liza, we're still looking for Mr. Goodbar," said Judy.

"So here you all are," I summed up, "running a small-time, low-profit stunt show in Forrest City, barely earning pork and bean money – yet Stark Enterprises is trying to buy you out. What have you got that he's so anxious to grab for himself?"

Judy sighed. "That's the big question. And we just don't have the answer. As I said back in Los Angeles, I was hoping *you* could find out what's behind Stark's offer."

"Could he be after the land?" asked Cahill.

"Naturally, we thought of that," said Liza. "But there's nothing here."

"Big highway coming through?" I asked. "Oil potential? Shopping center planned?"

Lyn giggled. "There's sure no oil around here. And no expressways or shopping centers either. Not in Forrest City."

Cahill shook his head. "There's *something* you people have overlooked. It's just a matter of finding out what."

The trailer door banged open and Uncle Jack entered, looking grim.

"I was out checkin' the equipment," he said. "Stark put one over on us."

Judy's eyes flashed. "What's happened?"

"One of his boys must have doubled back after the fight – when nobody was watchin' the cars. Got to the engines an' used acid. Nothin' left but scrap metal."

Liza slammed a fist against the table. "That cuts it! It took a bank loan to get us this far. We're all out of credit."

"We sure can't afford three more engines," said Lyn. "Ben Stark's got us beat."

"Not necessarily," I said.

They all had their eyes on me. I was looking at Uncle Jack. "How's the engine in the service truck? They get to that?"

He shook his head. "Nope, truck's okay."

"Good. Cahill and I will need to borrow it for a little trip tomorrow."

Mike cocked an eyebrow. "What's on your mind, Nick?"

I yawned, stood up, stretching. "Right now, pardner, sleep is on my mind."

The next day was Sunday and the town's main street was quiet as King Tut's tomb. All the shops were closed. Two old geezers sat on a bench playing checkers and taking in the sun. At the end of the second block I found the store I was looking for.

Cahill was driving the service truck and I told him to pull over in front of R. Butler's War Surplus.

"Now I know what happened to Rhett Butler after he left Scarlett," Mike said. "He opened a war surplus store in Forrest City."

I walked to the shop door, banged my fist against it. Above us, a window opened and a man leaned out. He was scowling. "It's Sunday, the Lord's day, an' we're closed. So quit poundin' on my damn door!"

"I'm Mel Purvis," I said. "With BIF. This is official business."

He blinked down at me. "BIF? What's that?"

"Bureau of Infiltration and Fabrication," I said briskly. "Sub branch of the CIA. You'd better get your ass down here, citizen."

The window closed. Heavy, descending footsteps from the inside stairs. A rattle of keys. The door opened. Butler looked like a disturbed bear; he was big and fierce-featured. His hair was ruffled, standing out from his head at odd angles. He'd probably been taking a snooze.

I flashed a fake wallet badge and stepped past him into the shop. Cahill followed.

"We'll need a few things," I told Butler. "Emergency requisition."

"Damn the U.S. Government," muttered Butler. But he looked resigned.

The bluff was working.

The trip from Forrest City to Ben Stark's fairground headquarters in Darlington took longer than we'd counted on, but we got there before dark. The main gate was locked, and the day's show was over. We flashed the guard some fake ID and he waved us past.

Stark put on all of his local stunt shows here at the Darlington Fairgrounds – a class act all the way. This was the Barnum and Bailey Circus in comparison to the Helle sisters' underfinanced effort. Hotter cars, bigger ramps, fancier stunts. A lot more of everything.

Cahill drove past the rows of empty grandstands to the garage area. We opened the truck doors and stepped out gingerly, like a pair of astronauts stepping onto the surface of the moon. We even looked like them in our full-body firesuits topped with large opaque-bubble helmets.

The garage area was swarming with mechanics working on the stunt vehicles, and they all stopped abruptly to stare at the two of us.

Their boss, a tall, blunt-faced guy sporting a shaved bullet head, walked over to us, followed by his top boy, who was smaller, with hangdog eyes.

"What's this all about?" asked bullethead.

"Emergency," I said through the speaker in my helmet. "Who are you?"

"I'm Ed Stricker, section chief, and this is Roe Collins, our head mechanic. Now, who the hell are you?"

"We're DTE. Department of Toxic Elements. We're checking out an alert in this area."

"What kind of alert?" Stricker looked sour and suspicious.

"It could be serious," I said. To Cahill: "What are you getting?"

Mike was holding up an electrical timing device we'd found in Butler's store (along with the firesuits). It began a steady clicking. "We've got an extremely high megatrobe count. Up to four thousand emps and rising."

"I think we have a severe situation here," I told Stricker. "This whole area is badly contaminated."

"You tellin' me the air's poisoned?"

"That's correct, sir. An anti-layer of active mega particles has drifted into stasis, causing an inverse strobe reaction. Please open your mouth."

He blinked uneasily. "What for?"

I took the timer from Cahill and held it close to Stricker's face. "I need to measure your megatrobe body count. Just open wide so I can get a reading."

He did that.

"Tongue out," I said. "Way out."

The device clicked against his thick pink tongue. I nodded.

"Lucky thing for you we got here when we did. You're into a hyper critical megatrobe bodycount. I'll have to ask you to evacuate the area immediately."

"Right," nodded Cahill. "You don't play games with megatrobe buildup."

"But we've got a show to do tomorrow!"

"Not until we've detoxified the area. I have to insist that you and your crew clear out at once. Walk out now."

"Walk?"

"That's correct. We can't allow any metallic objects to leave the area. No cars or trucks. You'll have to exit on foot. You can return within twelve hours. Should be perfectly safe here by then."

"This is all crazy," protested Stricker. "I never heard of—"

"Let me put it to you in basic terms," I said. "Either you leave now or you – along with your entire crew – will suffer a total testicular loss."

"What's that mean?"

"Once a maximum megatrobe body level is reached the male testicles revert to a shrunken walnut-like shape and then dissolve completely."

Roe Collins spoke for the first time: "You mean, we could lose our balls?"

"That is exactly what I mean, Mr. Collins."

That did it. Within minutes Stricker and Collins and their entire crew were hotfooting it for the exit gate. We began hosing down all the cars and trucks, using insecticide from two spray tanks found at Butler's store.

When Stark's men were out of sight we tossed the hoses

aside, stripped off our firesuits, and drove our truck to the rear of the main service garage.

Which was, by now, totally deserted. Tools lay where they had fallen; hoods were up, engines abandoned. Our warning had come across loud and clear.

A half hour later we left the Darlington Fairgrounds with what we'd come for, laughing and slapping at each other like a pair of happy hyenas.

It had been a truly satisfying afternoon.

When we drove up to the house trailer (Helletrailer?) all three sisters and Uncle Jack were outside waiting for us. I had refused to tell them what our plan was, so they had no idea of what we had in the truck. We were grinning broadly as we climbed out.

"You two cats look like you just swallowed the canary," said Judy. She was wearing an orange-sun tank top and pre-faded jeans and looked cute as a button. The kind of girl I should marry and settle down with but am not ready for yet. Private detectives should stay single. Saves divorce expenses. It's a rotten game for a wife and kiddies.

Cahill opened the rear doors of the service truck and stepped back as the others crowded forward for a look inside.

"Wow!" exclaimed Lyn.

"Terrific!" added Liza. "Three brand-new engines!"

"Replacements," I said, "courtesy of Ben Stark Enterprises. Now, Mr. Stark didn't personally authorize their delivery, but I'm sure he'd want you to have them."

"Absolutely," agreed Mike.

Judy giggled. "But, naturally, you didn't ask him."

"Naturally," I nodded.

"You stole 'em," said Uncle Jack, slapping his thigh in delight. "You up and damn well stole the lot!"

"I'd prefer to say that we...appropriated them," I said, winking at Mike.

"They were just sitting there, all crated up, in Stark's garage," Cahill stated. "Just begging to be used. Besides, he'll never miss 'em. Who's going to look inside three empty crates?"

"I'm not going to ask how you two characters managed to *do* this," said Judy. "All I care about is getting these three babies hooked up and running in time for our next show."

"Let's get cracking," said Uncle Jack.

The service truck's hoist was put to work, lifting out the acid-ruined engines and lowering the new ones into place. The three gleaming new powerplants were bolted tight, wires and hoses attached, then fired into roaring life. They made a sweet sound.

The Helledrivers were definitely back in business.

The show that weekend was a solid success. No trouble. No problems. Mike was probably right about Stark's boys not wising up to the fact that three of their engine crates were now empty. We'd pushed those suckers well back into the far corner of the garage. I mean, totally out of sight. Of course, the loss would eventually be discovered but, for the moment, there was no reason for Stark to connect us to the two helmeted DTE men. Certainly Stricker and Collins didn't suspect we were there to collect three engines; they were just grateful to hang onto their balls.

After the last show wrapped on Sunday we had another confab over coffee and doughnuts inside the trailer.

"You ladies put on a terrific act out there today," Mike told them.

Judy mock-bowed. "Thank you, kind sir!"

I agreed with Mike. "And the turnout was fabulous. A full house."

"Maybe they were expecting another punchout," said Liza. She sighed. "It can't last. Stark's bound to pull something else. It's just the calm before the storm."

"There goes Miss Negative," said Lyn. "Why don't you zip it up, Liza. We don't need more negativity right now."

Liza frowned. "At least I'm no Pollyanna like you. I look at things realistically. Stark's gonna nail our ass and you *know* it!"

"All I know is I'm sick of hearing you weep and wail about how bad things are. Maybe you've lost your guts, is that it, Liza?"

Judy pushed back her coffee cup and raised a calming hand. "Okay, you two, that's enough. I know we're all a little spooked about how well things went this weekend – but it could just be that Ben Stark is getting the idea that we're tough nuts to crack. Maybe he's backed off."

Liza was still sulking. "Sure, and maybe the moon's made of raspberry jello – but I wouldn't bet on it."

Lyn was glaring at her sister when the phone rang. Judy answered: "Yes? You're what?... Yes, okay, hold on a minute." Cupping a hand over the mouthpiece, she swung toward us. "It's Uncle Jack. His car broke down and he's stuck out at the junction of Sylmer Road and Langley."

"I know where that is," said Liza. "Tell him I'll be out to pick him up in the service truck."

Judy told him, then put down the phone, frowning. "He said he was phoning from a bar called 'The Good Life' out near the junction."

"So?" I said. "Something wrong with that?"

"I guess not," Judy said slowly. "It's just that Uncle Jack hates that place. He never goes there." She paused. "It's owned by Ben Stark."

"Well, he had to call from *someplace*," Cahill pointed out.

"You sure it was your uncle's voice?" I asked.

She nodded. "I'd know if it wasn't."

"I'll be going with Liza," I told Mike. "Just to be on the safe side."

"Want me with you?"

"No, I want you here with Judy and Lyn. In case Stark's men show up again. Remember, we're bodyguards."

"And I can't think of nicer bodies to guard," said Mike.

"Well, I'm bushed," Lyn admitted. "Me for some sack-time."

"You go on," said Judy. "Mike and I will watch the Late Show. It's a Bogart movie. The one where he's a gangster trapped in the mountains."

"That's *High Sierra*, and it's a knockout," I said.

"Walk soft," Mike told me. "Could be trouble out there."

"Trouble is my business," I said.

"And good night to you, Mr. Marlowe," smiled Lyn. I went out to the truck with Liza.

Sylmer Road was a bitch. Dark and narrow, lined by heavy trees, and bumpy as a toad's back. One of those old resurfaced Southern goat trails that pass for roads in this part of the state. Even the potholes had potholes. Liza was driving, and she didn't slow down for the curves; she knew the area and booted the truck along Sylmer like a galloping mustang. My back teeth were rattling by the time we reached the junction at Langley.

Suddenly...blam! A huge tree trunk slammed down directly in front of us across the road. Liza hit the brakes, and the truck slewed sideways, banging into the tree and knocking out our left headlight.

"Back it out!" I yelled. And Liza jammed the truck into reverse. Too late.

With another loud crash, a second tree dropped across the road, this one behind us, locking us in.

I had my .38 in hand by the time Liza cut the engine. She was shaking as we sat in the silent truck with cricket sounds washing around us. There was the smell of damp earth and fresh-cut timber in the air.

It all fell into place: Stark had grabbed Uncle Jack and forced him to make the call, probably at gunpoint. Then they'd set up the ambush. Things were getting nasty.

"Stay here," I told Liza. "I'm going to have a look around."

I edged out of the truck, keeping the .38 up and ready.

"You got a flash in the glove compartment?" I asked.

She nodded, still shaking, and handed me a long metal flashlight. The beam was strong.

"Lock both doors," I said. "And sound the horn if anybody comes near you."

"Okay," she said.

I didn't know what to expect as I carefully probed the surrounding darkness with the flash. No sound. No movement.

Where were they?

I was maybe ten feet from the truck when a hand grabbed my wrist. A violent twist and the .38 went spinning. At the same moment something connected with the back of my skull with terrific force. Another tree trunk? I didn't have time to find out what hit me; I was too busy diving into a pool of black stars.

It was a long way to the bottom.

I opened my eyes to Mike Cahill's sweating face. I was in a hospital bed and Mike was standing beside me with one of his big Irish paws on my shoulder. He was asking me if I was okay.

"No," I groaned. "I'm *not* okay. My head feels like a Sherman tank rolled over it."

Judy and Lyn were standing behind Cahill, looking concerned.

I sat up and probed at my head with gentle fingers. There was a bandage, like a turban, wound around my skull.

"We got worried, me and the girls," said Cahill. "So we

drove out there to find you."

"How's Liza?" I asked.

"She's alive," said Mike, "but they worked her over some."

"Meaning *what*?"

"They broke both of her legs below the knees."

"Those bastards!"

"She won't be doing any stunt driving for awhile," Mike declared. And he handed me a note. "This was with Liza when we found her."

The note was typed, without a signature.

YOU PEOPLE NEEDED A LESSON SO WE GAVE YOU ONE. IF YOU DON'T GET SMART AND SELL OUT MORE THINGS WILL HAPPEN. BAD THINGS. IT IS UP TO YOU.

I leaned back into my pillow. "How does Stark figure he can get away with this?"

"He's got the law in his hip pocket," said Judy. "Besides, we don't have any real proof against him. I mean, no witnesses. Nothing."

"What about Uncle Jack? Is he okay?"

"He was hit on the head," said Lyn. "They dumped him next to you and Liza. He's got a concussion."

"How bad?" I asked.

"He's in a coma right now," Judy stated. "But the doctor says he'll come out of it soon. He's not critical."

"Well, he's a witness, isn't he? They kidnapped him, forced him to make that phone call, right?"

Lyn nodded. "With a knife at his throat."

"But he never saw their faces," added Judy. "They kept a blindfold on him the whole time."

"Damn!" I drove a fist into my pillow. "Stark's gonna be the one to learn a lesson. And that's a promise!"

"The doc says Liza will have to wear casts on both legs," Mike told me.

"And Uncle Jack won't be leaving the hospital for maybe another week," said Judy.

"Which pretty well wrecks our show this weekend," declared Lyn.

"I can fill in for your uncle," Cahill said. "I'm pretty good behind a mike. When I was a kid I used to bally for a traveling carnival in the Midwest."

"Well...I guess we *could* do the show," nodded Judy. "With just Lyn and me driving. Except for the Rolling Flyover. That's a three-car stunt."

"And it's the one the crowd comes to see," Lyn declared. "Our star act. We don't do it and they'll yell for their money back. And with Liza out there's no driver for the jump car."

Mike looked at me and grinned. "Sure there is," he said.

Sitting in Liza's stunt car, in a red leather driving suit, strapped in like a mummy, a crash helmet over my still-sore head, with the crowd yelling for action and Mike's voice crackling over the loudspeakers, I told myself I was insane, nuts, bonkers, zonked out, to be doing what I was about to do.

What the hell did I know about stunt driving – let alone stunt *jumping*? Cahill was the one who jumped the overpass when Stark's boys were on our tail. He should be here, filling in for Liza, not me. But I'd been dumb enough to say yes, and now here I was being brave and stupid.

Actually, I felt anything but brave. But I did feel stupid. Judy, dressed in her racing leathers, was at my driving window, giving me some last-minute advice.

"Just be sure to keep your wheels straight when you're in the air. If they're at an angle when you land on the other ramp you could flip the car and that could be dangerous."

"Dangerous!" I moaned. "I feel like I'm in a rolling death trap!"

"You're just nervous. Everything will go fine. Look, Lyn is waving at me. I gotta get going."

"I'd ask you to deliver the eulogy at my funeral," I told her, "but I promised Mike he could do it."

She smiled and punched my shoulder. "Break your bones!" In racing terms it meant have a good ride.

"I *hate* that phrase," I said – but she was gone, on the way back to her car.

Then I was listening to Mike's dread words amplified over the stands: "…the spectacular…deadly…death-defying…Rolling Flyover!"

I pulled down my goggles, revved the engine (a pride of lions under the hood) and rolled into position on the field next to Lyn and Judy. They gave me a thumbs-up, then roared away as I gunned for the high wooden ramp.

Below me, the two Helle sisters made a wide loop near the grandstands, then headed straight for each other as I topped the first ramp.

I had to "fly" over them as they did their double flips below me – and I didn't have any more time to think about danger. Almost magically, I was off the edge and into the air (wheels straight!), aimed at the lip of the far ramp, swooping over the cars of Lyn and Judy. With a jarring *whump*, I landed on the other ramp, sailed down it, and hit the brakes, sliding sideways. The car spun like a top. Was I going to flip? No, I looped to a full stop, killing the engine – and the crowd went ape. They figured my wild spinout as part of the stunt.

The Helle sisters helped drag me out of the car, both of them giggling like schoolgirls.

"You were terrific!" enthused Judy.

"Outstanding!" Lyn declared.

"I used to think you people were crazy, pulling stunts like this," I told them, above the crowd noise. "I don't think so any more. Now I *know* you're crazy."

We all took a deep bow toward the stands, raising our arms in triumph. Then we hugged each other.

Showbiz.

Over the next few days I stayed close to Judy and Lyn, continuing to play bodyguard while Mike worked on a new angle for us. He'd been making a play for Ben Stark's housemaid, a cute little ash-blonde named Cecile. And she really seemed to dig him.

Stark lived in an expensively-restored Colonial mansion in the Darlington area with two house guards, a cook, a gardener, a houseman, and the maid, Cecile.

We needed inside info on Mr. S. – anything we could get that might prove of value to us – so Mike played Don Juan with little Cecile, taking her out for beer and a T-bone at a posh steak house in Darlington.

Which is when we found out about the map. Of the Forrest County region. Stark kept it locked away in a safe in his study, but Cecile had seen it once, when he had it out on his desk. She told Mike that the fairgrounds area, home of the Helledrivers, had been circled in red – but she hadn't been able to make out any details.

What she'd told Mike was enough. I was certain that the map would tell us why Ben Stark was so damned intent in getting his sleazy hands on the Helle property.

Next step: getting a close look at it.

Three days later. I was crouched on a hill behind a screen of heavy brush, observing Stark's place through a pair of high-power binocs. Mike was with me. We'd left Judy and Lyn at the hospital, visiting with Liza and Uncle Jack. They'd be safe there until we could get back to them. Mike had learned from Cecile that this was the servants' day off. No cook or gardener or houseman – and no Cecile. All we had to worry about was the one guard inside the house. The second guard stayed at the gate where he wouldn't bother us.

It was now late afternoon, with the sun casting long arms of shadow. Mike was on the binocs and he nudged me and handed me the glasses. "That white job. It's him in the back."

Stark's heavy, scrolled-iron gate slid open – activated by the guard – and a shiny swan-white Lincoln stretch limo eased from the house road onto the street. I could see Stark sitting in the back seat as the Lincoln whispered off beyond the trees.

The house was ours!

Well, not quite yet – since we had to get over the wall and take care of the inside guard. But we had no real trouble doing either. As Mike told me, the cosmic vibrations were sympathetic to us.

The wall was topped with daggered fragments of glass embedded in concrete, but we used a heavy canvas tarp to blunt the edges and slipped over with no sweat.

When we got to the house the inside guard was outside – smoking a joint on the wide, pillared veranda. Mike sent him to dreamland with a single neck chop. Neat and swift.

Once we were inside, we headed for the study. "Cecile told me the safe is behind a painting of Robert E. Lee," said Cahill. "Stark's a Civil War nut. He's got a whole shitpile of books on the Confederacy."

The house was fit for a king, which was how Stark thought of himself. He'd done a first-class job of furnishing the place. A series of dramatic Civil War paintings lined the hall leading to the study. A pair of crossed cavalry swords were mounted above the door.

We found General Lee and, sure enough, the safe was right where Cecile said it would be.

Cahill has a variety of handy talents and he had this wall job open inside of five minutes – losing a bet with me that he could crack it in four. I put a hand inside the safe, probing until I heard the soft crackle of roiled parchment. The map.

We carefully spread out the roll of yellow parchment on

the large study desk, using paperweights to hold it open.

"It's an old Confederate map," Mike noted. "Maybe it's just part of his Civil War collection."

"Then how come he circled the middle area in red and wrote in the word 'fairgrounds'? That's the Helle property."

Cahill traced a finger over the circled area, stopping at a faintly penciled X. "What's this mean?"

I shrugged.

Then Mike exclaimed: "The letter! Maybe that'll explain the X."

"What letter?"

"Cecile told me she saw a letter with the map that also looked real old. I'll bet they're connected."

I went back to the safe and found it. In a time-darkened envelope. I took out the sheet of paper, unfolded it, read the words and nodded.

"Well?" asked Mike. "What's it say?"

"According to this letter the cross on the map marks the location of a Confederate gold shipment buried there during the last days of the war to keep it out of Yankee hands." I gave him a knowing look. "Now we know what Stark's been after."

"Then what's kept him from taking it? How come he doesn't just drive into the fairgrounds with his goon squad some dark night and dig it up? Why try to *buy* the land?"

"Because he doesn't know where to dig," I said. "This says the gold was buried just in front of a double-forked tree. And there aren't any more trees left. They were all bull-dozed for the fairgrounds."

Cahill's face suddenly lit up. "Jeez, I *know* where it is!" I stared at him. "How could you?"

"Judy talked to me about the problems they'd had getting rid of this one big tree. She said it had a double fork, and that part of the stump's still there, under their house trailer. *That's* where the gold is buried."

A voice from behind us: "Thank you, gentlemen. I was sure that somehow you'd come up with the solution to my little problem. I am most appreciative."

We turned to face Ben Stark. Salter and Grady were standing on either side of him. Salter had a Colt Commander aimed at us, and Grady carried a pumpgun. Behind them, smiling like Lucrezia Borgia, was our little Cecile.

Cahill glared at her. "You bitch," he said softly. "You set us up."

"Indeed she did." Stark was chuckling. "You didn't really think it would be this easy, did you? Just hop the wall, knock over a guard, open the safe, and there's the map. I'm not that big a fool."

"You have been up to now," I said pleasantly. "I had no reason to think you'd change."

He ignored this, turning to Salter. "You know what to do with them."

The clown poked his Colt into my short ribs. "Move, boyo. Start walking."

And we walked.

Our destination turned out to be a basement storage room full of mold and darkness. They shoved us inside. The air was foul.

"I was hoping for nicer quarters," I told Salter. "This room is downright unsanitary."

"You're lucky I don't put a bullet through your head, smart guy," Salter growled. "And, later, maybe I will."

"Pluggin' these two would be a real kick," said Grady, keeping the pumpgun on us. "One fer you and one fer me."

"Ben'll probably want to do the job himself," declared Salter. "Soon as he gets back from his treasure hunt."

And they slammed the storage door shut, locking it. "What now?" asked Cahill.

"We bust out of here."

"What with – our fingernails? That's a solid oak door. And it's bolted from the outside."

"Trust me," I said, walking to the far end of the room. A barred window was set flush with the outside yard at grass level. A pale glow of dying afternoon sun penetrated the dust-filmed glass.

"We go out here," I said.

Cahill tried the window. "It's locked. And even if it wasn't, how do we melt through those bars?"

"You're supposed to have faith in the cosmos," I told him. "Me, I feel these good vibrations!"

"You're putting me on, Nick."

"We have a choice. We can wait here till Stark gets back and have him shoot us or we can get the hell out that window."

"So now you're Blackstone the Magician," Mike said. "Okay, okay, show me what you've got up your sleeve."

"Actually, it's under my armpit." And stripping off my shirt I raised my left arm and peeled away a wide band of flesh-colored tape. Then I held out a thin, tapered-steel chisel. "When Salter patted me down he missed this little beauty," I said. "Ideally designed for emergency exits."

Mike was grinning. "Dammit, Nick, it's like you keep tellin' me – you *are* brilliant."

I got serious. "Here's the plan… There's a shelf above the door. Climb up there and wait. I'll try not to make any more noise than I have to but if Salter hears me working on the window he's going to come in here to see what's happening. That's when you land on his neck. I'll grab his gun. Once we have that we can deal with Grady. Okay?"

"I love it," Mike said.

While he climbed up to his perch I got to work, popping the window lock with the chisel and driving its sharp steel tip into the concrete holding the bars in place. It was just as I'd hoped; the stuff was old and began to crack and crumble. We'd be out in no time at all.

But Salter heard me, and came through the door with his gun leveled. "Get away from that window or I'll–"

He didn't get a chance to finish his threat. Like a big, grinning Irish monkey, Cahill dropped from the shelf to fasten his beefy hands around Salter's neck. A quick twist and the scuzzbag was down and out.

I scooped up the Colt as Grady came charging. He got off one blast from the pumpgun which tore a sizable hole in the wall next to my head before I was able to bring up the Colt and squeeze off two rounds. I placed both shots in his kneecaps.

He screeched like a stepped-on cat and dropped his weapon, clutching wildly at his legs as he fell to the floor.

"Oh, Jesus, it hurts! It hurts!"

He wouldn't be doing any marathon running for awhile.

With the door open, we headed back upstairs, both of us armed and ready for more of Stark's boys. But the house was quiet; apparently the whole gang was out at the fairgrounds digging for Confederate gold.

We walked through the kitchen to Stark's five-car garage. And there was the shiny white stretch limo.

"I'll hot-wire this mother and we can use it to get to the fairgrounds," said Mike.

He started toward the Lincoln, but I put a hand on his arm. "No good. We'd just be running into more than we could handle. Too many guns." I looked around the garage. "Let Stark come back here with the gold and we'll prepare a little reception in his honor."

Mike looked at me. "What kind of a reception?"

I just smiled.

In Viet Nam, Mike had been trained as a demolitions expert, and his skill had been amply demonstrated when he blew away Stark's speedboat. I'd noted a box of explosive charges stacked against the back wall. God knows what they were for, but Ben Stark was a man who enjoyed destruction and I was happy to use his own equipment to provide some.

It took Mike the better part of an hour to carry out my instructions, and by then it was dark. We didn't switch on any lights; that would have warned Stark. We just sat there in the darkness until we heard the sound of cars coming up the drive to the house.

Mike checked the window. "The ogre returns to his castle."

"Just in time for his royal homecoming."

Something had gone wrong at the fairgrounds. Stark looked mean as a pit bull as he left his Mercedes and mounted the veranda. And his boys didn't look any happier. Nobody was smiling.

"They didn't find it," I told Mike. "No gold."

"Yankees probably dug it up after the war," Cahill declared. "All those years and Ben's treasure turns out to be a pipe dream. Talk about poetic justice."

"He's coming in," I said, ducking behind a fold of hanging velvet drapery. "It's party time!"

The front door opened and Stark walked into the foyer, followed by his muscle boys, four of them. He paused, looking around. "Salter!" he yelled. Silence. "Grady!" More silence. He scowled darkly. "Where *are* those stupid assholes?"

"They're not available," I said, stepping from behind the drapes with Salter's Colt Commander in my hand.

"Yeah," said Mike, standing next to me with Grady's pumpgun up and ready. "Said something about early retirement."

"So you two pissers are loose, eh?" said Stark.

"Since you seem to own the local fuzz," I said, "we decided to put in a call to the State Police. They're on the way here to pick you boys up on a colorful variety of charges. So just put all your cannons on the floor."

Stark turned to his goon squad; he was smiling. "You heard the man. He wants us to surrender our weapons." Then he gave me a hard stare. "I'd say you're suffering from a severe self-destruction complex."

I warned him: "Go for us and you won't like what happens."

But Stark sent his four-man army into motion – and they hit the first set of trip wires.

The library exploded into fragments and flame. "There goes your Civil War book collection," I taunted, ducking toward the study. "You'd better call off the hounds."

"Get those bastards!" Stark bellowed.

At the end of the hall they hit the second trip wire, and the rear section of the house went up in a fountain of ruptured beams and falling plaster.

"That was your gourmet kitchen," I shouted, staying out of firing range. "Call 'em off, Stark, or the whole house goes – and you with it!"

Stark knew I was telling it true. His face was the color of chalk and his hands were shaking. He looked at his men. "Do what he said, put down your guns." And he put his own pearl-handled .45 on the hallway floor. The other four followed his example.

He turned toward us and slowly raised his arms in the air. "You win."

I walked over to him. "This is for what you did to Liza," I said. And I laid the barrel of the Colt across his left cheek, splitting the skin. The blow drove him into the wall.

A thin, wailing sound rose above the crackle of flames. Sirens.

"You're right," I said. "We win."

When we got back to the fairgrounds the house trailer was

turned over, lying on its side in the glare of our headlights like a broken toy discarded by the Jolly Green Giant. Stark had rammed it with a couple of his big trucks to clear the ground for his treasure hunt.

On the way over we'd stopped off at the hospital to spread the good news of Stark's arrest. Uncle Jack got so excited he almost fell out of bed and Liza said she felt like kicking up her heels (but her casts were too heavy).

Judy and Lyn had come back with us to the fairgrounds and now they gazed sadly at the devastated trailer. "*Now where do we sleep?*"

"Those lousy stinkers!" sighed Judy. "I hope they rot in prison!"

Our flashlights revealed the tree stump; there was a large hole in front of it. A metal strongbox had been pulled from the raw earth and its rusted lock broken open. We looked inside.

"No wonder Stark was so pissed," I said. Lyn giggled. "It's full of Confederate bills."

"Worthless as paper," added Cahill. "Ole Ben, he sure went to a lot of trouble for nothing."

Judy shook her head. "He may have collected Civil War stuff, but obviously he didn't know his history."

She picked up a discarded shovel and began scooping out the soft earth at the bottom of the hole. The blade of the shovel rang on metal.

"The Confederates had a habit that Ben Stark wasn't aware of," she said. "They buried their gold *under* their currency."

She was right. There was a second strongbox – and *this*

one was packed with gold bars. Dozens of solid gold bars. I held one up, hefting it in my hand.

"Mike me boy," I said. "I think this case is going to pay off for us after all."

And he gave me a wide Irish grin.

One thousand trade paperback copies of *Ships in the Night* were printed by Capra Press in 2004. Twenty-six copies in slipcases have been lettered and signed by the author.

ABOUT CAPRA PRESS

Capra Press was founded in 1969 by the late Noel Young. Among its authors have been Henry Miller, Ross Macdonald, Margaret Millar, Edward Abbey, Anais Nin, Raymond Carver, Ray Bradbury, and Lawrence Durrell. It is in this tradition that we present the new Capra: literary and mystery fiction, lifestyle and city books. Contact us. We welcome your comments.

155 Canon View Road, Santa Barbara, CA 93108
www.caprapress.com

WILLIAM F. NOLAN

With eighty books to his credit, William F. Nolan is a prolific, multi-genre master whose works have been selected for more than three hundred anthologies and textbooks, including many "Best of the Year" volumes. Among a host of honors, Nolan has been cited for excellence by the American Library Association, is twice winner of the Edgar Allan Poe Special Award, and was named an official "Living Legend" by the International Horror Guild in 2002. He has also written extensively for films and television and has won Golden Medallion television awards at two European film festivals.

Nolan's best-selling global classic, *Logan's Run* (a million copies sold in the United States alone), spawned a hit MGM film and a CBS television series, and there are now two dozen active Logan websites around the world. Warner Bros. is currently in pre-production on a new, mega-budget, major film version of *Logan's Run*.

Nolan lives in Southern California with his writer-wife Cameron Nolan, two cats, two parakeets, ten thousand books, and a stuffed gorilla. He plans to retire from writing on his hundredth birthday.